CRITICAL ACCLAIM FOR EVELYN CONLON

Taking Scarlet as a Real Colour

'Conlon's is an original voice: an articulation of a strong feminine sensibility that takes its place in the new tradition of Irish writing.'
Erica Wagner, *The Times*

'Conlon is a fine writer, as well as a woman of strongly held convictions. Her characters are articulate, passionate and frequently funny, and much of her prose is a delight in itself.'
Sunday Times

'a first-rate collection full of original insights and characters'
Publishers Weekly

'an enjoyable, intriguing and above all challenging read'
Irish Post

'a genuinely exploratory writer, true to every kink which her imagination puts into her characters . . . her work is excitingly original'
Irish Times

A Glassful of Letters

'Meticulously observant . . . Conlon writes with sane, sober wit; her lucid prose is pithy without falling into epigrams . . . Her account of contemporary Ireland and the continuing Irish diaspora is sympathetic, well-measured and insightful.'
Publishers Weekly

'Conlon succeeds in delivering a highly vibrant, contemporary perspective . . . [she] has struck a seam of complexities and contradictions buried within the apparently mundane.'
Irish Studies Review

EVELYN CONLON was born in 1952 in County Monaghan. She lived for a number of years in Australia and travelled extensively in Asia. Her short stories have appeared in many publications and anthologies. She has published two volumes of stories and two novels, the last of which, *A Glassful of Letters*, was published by Blackstaff Press in 1998. She was a recipient of Arts Council Bursaries for Literature in 1988 and 1995. She has been writer in residence in Dublin City Library and counties Kilkenny, Cavan and Limerick. She now lives in Dublin.

telling
new and selected stories

evelyn conlon

THE
BLACKSTAFF
PRESS

BELFAST

First published in 2000 by
The Blackstaff Press Limited
Blackstaff House, Wildflower Way, Apollo Road
Belfast BT12 6TA, Northern Ireland
with the assistance of
The Arts Council of Northern Ireland

ARTS
COUNCIL
of Northern Ireland

Typeset by Techniset Typesetters, Newton-le-Willows, Merseyside

Printed in Ireland by ColourBooks Limited

A CIP catalogue record for this book
is available from the British Library

ISBN 0-85640-673-2

www.blackstaffpress.com

for my sisters
Bríd, Cecelia and Teresa

ACKNOWLEDGEMENTS

Some of these stories have appeared before in the author's own collections: *My Head Is Opening* (Attic Press, 1987) and *Taking Scarlet as a Real Colour* (Blackstaff Press, 1993). Others have been published in the *Sunday Tribune*, *Bad Sex*, *God*, *Serpent's Tail*, *Sceptre Short Stories*, *Trans-Continental* (Paris), *Nouvelles d'Irlande* (Quebec), *Irishe Short Stories* (Stuttgart), *Cimarron Review* (USA), *Journal of Irish Literature* (USA), *Midland Review* (USA) and *Fiction International* (USA). Several have been broadcast on BBC Radio. 'Taking Scarlet as a Real Colour' was performed in the Edinburgh Theatre Festival.

I would like to thank Fintan, Warren, Trevor and my friends who have made my life lively over the years that these stories were being written.

CONTENTS

A night out 1

Telling 17

The sound of twin 22

The park 31

Taking scarlet as a real colour,
  or And also, Susan 45

The long drop 58

A little remote 67

The tour 82

According to Michael 94

The undeathing of Gertrude 103

Two good times 112

On the inside of cars 118

Furthermore, Susan 130

Beatrice 137

Birth certificates 152

Petty crime 179

Park-going days 193

The last confession 202

Escaping the Celtic Tiger,
  world music and the millennium 212

A NIGHT OUT

We did finally find her, actually I found her, but no one believed me when I told them why she had run away from us. They shouldn't have been expected to believe me, it wasn't the sort of thing that came up in their conversations with their husbands or their wives every day, or month, for that matter, but I had thought that her standing among us had been such a solid thing that they could have bent themselves forward or sideways enough to let her actions become part of the normal happening of a life. But after the first pangs of missing they had felt a necessity to forget her, almost kill her off, because her behaviour had been so outrageous and had risen their adrenalins in such waves of condemnation that, even when their blood pressures had returned to normal, they couldn't let her back in, because if they did, why then had they lost their heads so in the first place? And also, they would have each remembered what the others had said, so all of them would have felt a little hypocritical if they'd backed down the moral mountain. I had always kept an airwave in my head clear for her and I suspected that some of the others secretly thought fondly of her at odd moments.

We were having one of our rare, unplanned reunions, things had happened, people were visiting, someone decided to risk another night, having forgotten any lingering distaste from the last one. It was Angela who had rung my wife. Arrangements were made – dinner in the Trocadero, our favourite. We couldn't get ourselves enthusiastic about the new, glitzier places, where you might see famous faces. We preferred the one restaurant that was part of our shared pasts. No one could overpose there. In a different restaurant someone might have shown too much familiarity with the sort of place that was beyond the pockets of some of us. We liked the fullness of the meals, too, the private memories of our first Sambucas there, the sort of purity that could attach itself to us from the time before we had made compromises, cheated, did crooked business deals, turned our backs. The Trocadero it was.

Everyone came, all eight of us, that is, four and our partners, no loose ends, although two of the partners were second time around. We didn't just imagine it, we were pleased to see each other; we looked alike, content enough, any serious problems put away for the night and, with luck, maybe for longer, after we would flash our lives around a bit across the table. Not doing too bad, really. We were well satisfied with ourselves towards the end of the meal when I mentioned Norah. I had wanted it to be a real surprise; well, it was. We never thought we'd hear from, or about, her again; that is, if she was still alive. We had known that she was still alive at one stage two years after her departure but had heard no definite word since. I began.

'Well, guess who I bumped into?'

'Who?' someone asked too quickly, not giving the others time to think.

'Guess,' I said again, but it wasn't going to work, there could be any number of people that we all knew.

'Norah,' I said. 'Norah. In Paris I met Norah.'

'Who?' someone shrieked, as if I'd said death herself.

'Norah? You mean, Norah Dinkin,' someone's husband said in a voice that was a few tones lower.

'Yes, Norah Dinkin.'

Well, well, well. The silence was too long, as each of them weighed up whether to let curiosity win over contempt.

'And what did she have to say for herself?' Lillian asked, allowing sufficient sharpness to cling to the words so that she could not be accused of having forgiven her.

'Well, of course, she was surprised to see me too.'

'I bet!'

I told them that she looked well and was working as a translator. She had always been great at languages, used to get me into such a storm of envy – that nimble facility around alien words, dance with them, she did.

'She lives in –'

'Who with?' Lillian asked.

'With whom?' her husband said.

'Oh shut up,' she said, delighted to be back on the home ground of intimate put-down.

Everyone played for time, while letting the ghost of Norah hover, unsure what to do with her. I forged ahead.

When we had first met, not all together on the same night, but certainly in the same year, we were in the habit of asking, 'Where do you come from?'

Norah would answer, 'Don't know, but I know how I got in' – she would leave a second's silence – 'through the bathroom window.'

She kept this reply up long enough to stop people asking, but not so long that any of us had to moan. Still, we never forgot it, nor what it was meant to mean. But it was OK because lots of us were doctoring a thing or two here and there, nineteen was the age to do it – maybe make your mother a little less anxious, your father all round more bearable, use distance as gloss. We were up in Dublin studying, everyone said 'up', even the northerners; no one said 'over' or 'back'. Most of us would be the next Dubliners, or certainly would have the next generation of them, but that was far from our minds at the time. Every crowd has to have a mascot, which they call the life and soul of the party. Norah was ours. Of course, they're often the people with blackspots for memory. 'Don't overdo complaining about clichés,' she'd say, 'it will stop you getting flowers.'

We went to dances, discos, clubs. We had catholic tastes. Sometimes we were happy; sometimes the men huddled together checking the talent. One would see someone that he liked the look of, he would turn to the others to solicit opinion, but in so doing would make himself nervous and uncertain. He would do this a few times, adding complications onto doubt, making himself noticeable, and eventually one of his mates would ask her to dance first. If that man then married her, it would be forgotten that Johnnie had spied her first. It's no wonder that years later we sometimes felt shocking, unexplained *frissons* going on between the wrong wives and husbands. Other nights we would be relaxed and sidle in and out of the most extraordinary confidences. Somehow we got our girlfriends and boyfriends, long after Norah, of course, who had already plunged in and, rumour had it, was sleeping not only with her boyfriend but with others as well. We didn't believe it and hadn't the nerve to ask her. Maybe we didn't want to know, because, in truth, we rather liked the rumour of it, it brought a certain undeserved reputation to our crowd.

We got married in or around the same year, we sneaked up the aisles of chapels as virgins, more untruthful steps rarely taken. Norah got married too. Some of us were surprised at her doing such an ordinary thing, but we were pleased to notice that she was leading the same life as the rest of us. Nothing could have been further from the truth, she told me in the café in Paris. I had suggested coffee, but while we were settling our seats nervously, me suddenly afraid, I was sorry that I hadn't suggested a drink.

'Maybe we should have a drink,' I said, but Norah didn't drink any more. I said, 'Really?' Her who used to turn up the sound of drunkenness.

'It's OK,' she said; 'not for ever, just for a month now and again, so I don't have to give up completely.'

We talked generally, remarked on our looks, our children. At the mention of them her mouth tightened.

'I see them now. Or should I say, I am allowed to see them now. Tom sends them over occasionally.'

She knew that I had become uncomfortable. An unspoken accusation lay heavily between us in the silence. I thought that she might be enjoying my discomfort. It was the only thing that I could think in self-defence.

'You didn't try to talk to us. To put your side.' I said weakly.

'I shouldn't have had to. If a person is in crisis, it's up to friends to help, not the other way about, surely.'

'Yes.'

I knew that she was right. But she claimed that our inadequacy had been useful in the end because it had forced her out of Ireland, and, boy, what a relief that had been.

We had tried not to take sides, but not very hard. Her husband got to our doorsteps first, and into our sitting rooms, and in no time at all he was following us around our kitchens, making tea for himself, recovering, and it seemed to be right. Or easier. Because not one sentence remained intact if it was said to both of them. Their understanding of language, punctuation, innuendo, had careered off in different directions.

Norah Dinkin hadn't come in the bathroom window. She had been born and reared like the rest of us – breakfast, dinner, tea, bed. But she had been bred in a severe loneliness. She wondered if hitting might have been easier, but no, she'd had a bit of that, too, and found it harder to coil in when there was pain on the skin as well.

But, as is mostly the case, she found a way for consolation. She took a lift home from a dance with a man whose name and appearance she knew. He touched her in places that she hadn't as yet located on herself, and he lay on top of her, well almost, he lay as on top of her as he could in the front seat of his minibus. He knew better than to suggest the back. In the loss of consciousness experienced she found her escape. She would never again cry, never conjure up the losses suffered as a result of the mind-numbing neglect that had passed as her childhood. It was an unfortunate trick to play on oneself, or was it? The oblivion of sleep heals too. She would flood the sore parts of her mind by touching and kissing men. What could be simpler, less harmful? It had been a shame to be so passively reflective about her loneliness, looking at people as if they were in a museum. Now that she had connected, her days, her appearance, would be different. The fact that another body could give such oblivion was a miracle. Her own body would occupy its ground less confusedly. The fact that placing such expectations upon kissing and touching might be a misunderstanding of the human condition and her role in it, mattered not. Finally there was *something*. And this had been her living guise when we had met her, a sleight of body that created its own acceptable level of untruth. How little we had known. And if she found her consolations with too many, so be it, who would know? She genuinely thought that Dublin was a big city, but wouldn't have worried even if it wasn't; she hadn't developed a sense of blame.

Dublin must have been big enough, because a lot of us didn't know just how extensive her experiences were. Certainly her husband didn't, she told me in Paris. But she gave it all up on the day of her marriage and innocently thought that the past had been rolled away with the red carpet. She thought that she wouldn't have to pay, because she had seen her promiscuity as a stipend due to her. Now all was square, she would give and be given in equal measure. She would have a chance to build downwards when they had children, and she did.

Her husband, Tom, worked with me for some years. He was a practical, novel man, given to unusual interpretations that brightened our Monday mornings, but which had usually run dry by Friday at four. I often felt that there was something sneaky about him, but my own wife said that I had it wrong, that I was a bad judge of character – 'Not that bad, of course,' she'd add, flirting like mad. She had come from a large midland town, where they got confidence earlier than in country villages, and she had always managed to stay that little bit ahead, even now in the city. 'Whatever you say, my dear.'

Tom got promotion before the rest of us. Either he and management had reached a non-verbal understanding, as they passed each other in the corridors, or the rest of us were too slow, or too busy being in love, or finding out if we believed there was such a thing, nibbling at adulthood. His promotion entailed a lot of travel, so, of course, one night he fell out of his matrimonial bed and didn't regret it enough not to do it again. The success of his treachery stunned him and gave him even more confidence. And further promotion. It was all his own doing, he reflected, and piled more confidence around himself. Soon people would have begun to hate him but for what happened next.

One night his bed pal floundered around the normal

conversation.

'Do you do this often?'

'No,' Tom lied, 'do you?'

'Not often nor well,' the woman said, shamelessly trying to kick-start a formula.

'Oh, you do it well enough,' Tom said, falling for it.

'Not as well as Norah Dinkin.'

'What do you mean, not as well as Norah Dinkin, who is Norah Dinkin?'

'Oh, just a girl I was at school with. She was great at getting fellas for more than kissing, so the rest of us used to say, if we were asked how we got on at the dance the night before, "Not as well as Norah Dinkin".'

'And where was this school?'

'Offaly.'

'Offaly. Where in Offaly?'

'Birr. Birr in Offaly.'

'Really. The Mercy, no doubt.'

'Yes, actually.'

'And where is Norah Dinkin now, do you think?'

'Oh married in Dublin. The usual.'

Tom didn't feel inclined to have sex again. He couldn't wait to get home.

Presumably it was the surprise of the question that caught Norah off guard, or maybe it was all those years that they had spent stacking up love together, and her never once unfaithful. Who would think that dead, unremembered acts could be a bulldozer waiting on the sidelines?

'How many?' Tom roared.

'I don't know, I honestly don't know.'

'Well start counting.'

'Ten, I suppose . . .'

The 'suppose' shocked him. Was she testing? Did she think

that ten might be acceptable?

'Ten! Ten! Some virgin!'

And then he remembered reading somewhere that when doctors ask patients how much they drink, they multiply the answer to reach the possible truth, by three for men, by eleven for women. And that was only drink.

'You were nothing but a slut.'

He was shocked himself by the sound of the word.

Tom told us all and we pitied him. We had forgotten the reputation ourselves, because Norah had become an exemplary wife and mother, an occasional fill-in teacher of French when friends of hers got sick. We remembered it now, enthusiastically, because despite the contentment of our days, in truth our lives needed a little gossip.

Tom and Norah did try. They went away for a weekend.

'We don't get on very well any more,' she said sadly and bravely.

'We do,' he said emphatically and dishonestly.

Tom travelled away more and more. Norah flinched and crawled for a year or so and then one night went to her local pub and made a pass at a man. Of course, he was separated, living with his mother again, heartbroken about his wife, and Norah couldn't take him home either, but they found a way. The man worked in the service industry, he said. He drove a Carlow-registered car and his hobby was abseiling. He told her fond words and that made a change. Norah told me that this was the dilemma. Would she, could she, use this as a crutch? Would it be enough for her to have the compliments of a security man ringing in her ears, words uttered on the spurs of moments in order to draw her in closer? They might be hard to remember. Could she call them up at necessary moments and swallow them in prescribed doses and would they pep her up enough to carry on? She knew that she would forget the orgasms, because lined up back to back they wouldn't make up that much time, but would the words help?

I wasn't used to this sort of conversation.

'But what about your marriage?' I asked, as if marriage truly was a piece of paper that could be consulted, verified, and adhered to.

'Oh, that was over,' she said. Her voice was low, final and definite, not for questioning. 'You see, he simply could not recover from the effort of altering my history, revisionism is hard work. We were so polite, so civil, not a bit like us, really. When you start saying "Thank You" every time one of you passes a cup of tea, you've had it. And what looks can say! You must know – the opposite is also true and you've been in love. No, it was over all right. All my domesticating blown away by one tart. Does the word shock you?'

And we discussed tarts, light-heartedly. I didn't mention this last bit in the Trocadero.

So she met the security man a second time, knowing that she didn't want to, knowing that it would do no good, but magneted somehow by the sound of his praise. A few days afterwards, she went to where they had gone on this second time. She left the house intending to go for a walk along her normal seaside route but took the turn instead down to the South Port, past the dead cranes, under the glassed gangway. The Travellers were still there, in their two caravans. The women had organised places for everything; the ditch behind had been scraped out to become staggered shelves.

She felt herself to be the object of her own actions. In her plaid suit, she walked past the place where he had manoeuvred her against the wall, kissed her, got his hand inside her bra, while she had thought, looking over his shoulder, half seeing the woman sitting in the car at the end of the pier, I'm not doing this, surely I'm not doing this.

'There's a woman in that car.'

'Where?'

He had turned to look. They had walked on and had come to what looked like a private spot. She hadn't wanted to go on, to let herself feel anything, but that day, too, she had been merely object, or was it subject? And which was the most frightening? No one seeing the woman in the suit would have matched that day to this. He had helped her to get over the wall, his hand held out like a pre-sixties gentleman, which he indeed was. He said something terrible, like 'Let's explore', or something even worse.

They had meandered behind the broken wall, and started then, a ridiculous groping. Although she had felt nothing in her heart, it was amazing how a body could go into automatic pilot, taking the certainty out of all those things it had thought it had felt for the special person, the best moment. It had been awkward; she hadn't wanted to take off her trousers, not even take them down far, it was too exposed, too awful. But she had an orgasm, a terrible thing, she thought. She had looked at her ring, gold was warmer than silver, a woman of her age usually had a set of both, but couldn't use the silver because the wedding ring must stay on.

Would she be able to find the spot? Was it here? Why was she looking? There it was, the exact spot. She had made a pilgrimage to nothing. There was a man walking just out of her vision. Was he, too, looking for a spot? Were all those people walking the pier together actually fooling each other, casting an eye to bits of grass behind the wall of the derelict house, or to spots of sand?

As she walked back she thought, God, we were very near that woman in the car. The New Irish Ferries ship was in the dock, you always saw ships here, natural, I suppose, Norah thought, like Catholics in Rome. On the way home, on that other day, she had been glad that she was driving, between that and the smoking, she had had plenty to do. He had been in a rush, because he was having his children to bring them to the match, to see the Boys in Green on the crest of their tsunami. 'They should have left home by now,' he had said, and the sadness of it all, mixed with the aftersex, nearly overwhelmed her. It was hard to keep her foot on the accelerator.

In the Trocadero I abbreviated all this down to a few sentences.

And there had been a third arrangement. Norah had her mind made up by now not to see him again, but, because of her years, and because of having seen the unnecessariness of public humiliation, she was too polite not to turn up this last time. She was coming from a day teaching French in Navan, and she drove too fast up the road. She overtook cars before the end of straight white lines, hit eighty in spots. She was determined to be there on time. Unfortunately she was on the Cavan road and had to cross over to Phibsboro at some point. Should she go to Slane? No, Ashbourne. She should have gone to Ratoath but missed the turn. There was a dual carriageway coming up – she would go down the Dublin–Navan Road and get there. She was a creature of time-keeping and therefore pleased to arrive at St Peter's church with five minutes to spare. She took a left, crossed Connaught Street and parked her car on the quiet part of Ulster Street, between Munster Street and Leinster Street.

Surprisingly, there was a bra in her washbag. She took it out and used it as a face cloth, did a quick hair settlement, sprayed some perfume, and put her bags in the boot. It would never do to have them stolen. How could they have been stolen while you were driving? Then she was, dispassionately, ready. She went into the pub next door to perform her toiletries. The clientele were so much not her sort, nor she theirs, that all faces swivelled towards her, as if they had lives apart from their owners, who did not want to be caught out being curious. My God, they would remember her, as people do in a murder enquiry. 'She was seen at five twenty-five in Madigan's of Phibsboro. It appears that she then went next door to The Hut bar where she met a man.' She slunk out, straightened herself, pulled her shoulder blades together, the way a turkey settles its wings, and stepped inside. There he was. She'd seen worse-looking, now that she could look at him.

'White wine spritzer,' she said.

'What? What's that?' he asked.

'It's OK. White wine, please.'

'We'll sit over here.'

'How are you?' she asked. How's your ex-wife, your mother, your children – she'd be asking him about his back in a minute. She had no interest in any of these things. He asked her nothing, of course.

'You know that this isn't worth it. I've booked into two hotels, and cancelled them. I'm afraid of the phone ringing. I think we should call it a day,' she said.

Easy.

He spent some time telling her how great she was, while she wondered detachedly if anyone had seen bits of their naked bodies down at the port. He was on night duty, but had paid someone to work for him until ten thirty. She wouldn't like to change her mind, would she? She hadn't by any chance booked anywhere this time?

It was easy to say no.

There were two young women in the corner, drowning in conversation, pulling this way and that, trying to make sense of the unreasonable. Funny how girlfriends usually wore some of the same things – these ones had similar desert boots, at least that's what they had been called last time around. And they

had jumpers tied around their waists – usually a sign of unhappiness at the size of one's bottom. At least this man had made
Norah feel OK on that score, hers was only a body like
everyone else's, it was what a person did with it that counted.

'Would you call those windows plate glass or what? Lovely
pub, the counter's real,' he said.

'When I first came to Dublin,' she said, 'I met a man at a bus
stop and made a date with him. I was to meet him here, but I
was afraid to tell the aunt, who was briefly putting me up. Bus
stops weren't acceptable places to meet men. So I went to
Doctor Zhivago with my friend Marina instead. He turned up
all right, and when I didn't, he went to my address and told
my aunt anyway.'

'So you always picked up men in strange places. At least you
turn up now, as if you did this all the time,' he said, wiping out
all those years of correct behaviour.

She was almost finished her wine, but he wanted another
drink, presumably hoping that one more would weaken her
resolve and lead to a different few hours than the ones he could
now see looming in front of him until he could go to work at
half past ten.

'Not for me, thanks,' she said, in a faked regretful voice.

'Well, I'll have one myself. Harp shandy, please. You can
leave before me,' he said.

As she stood up he grabbed her hand and said, 'Your husband's a lucky man.'

'Don't be ridiculous,' she said, 'that's not the way things
work, you know that.'

'Yes. Still, I'd give up a lot to have you around me.'

'Goodbye,' Norah said.

She presumed that parts of his body were hurting him.
Hers felt fine. She waved when she got to the door, a friendly
flick of her wrist. Once outside, she felt a joyous, young

sense of relief.

'I'll get rid of them all.' She decided.

It was clear now. Tom would never forgive her, simply never. And the older she got, the more lines that crept over her face, the looser her flesh became, the more he would blame her. She would end up being the cause of his mortality. She could not do it any longer. She wanted to be pure, to have no more interest in the cravings of the flesh than women in poems had. Or, at most, she wanted to desire fulfilment with a man who could interest her, and cope with her past. She wanted to be able to wait for minor satisfactions with someone also so inclined. She wanted not to be modern, never to think the word 'sex'. If she failed that, she would retire. That's how she saw it, a retirement.

And we knew the rest. The breakup, the child custody case, the dirt, wheelbarrows full of it, our own gradual turning away from such a mess. The custody case had not actually gone into the courtroom. The threat of exposure, of lists of names, which she had foolishly given to Tom in a flood of Gulag-type confession, was enough to make her give in on a Tuesday morning at ten o'clock in the corridor. For some weeks she had met other women like herself, one whose nerve had failed her, because she had slept with a woman. The consolation of mutual despair, the imagined view of the years to come, were an imprisonment in themselves. Booking a ticket out seemed a wiser thing to do. Bury the best part of herself and start speaking another language.

I, of course, wanted to know how she had lived, but too many things had happened over the years and the question seemed paltry and unsophisticated. It whistled past her. But she absent-mindedly said something about a year of black mornings, then one of brightening nights and dark mornings, and a third when the nights were normal and the mornings had dawns. She said that the children were coming over for Easter, had none of us known that? No, we'd lost contact with Tom as well. Funny, she had always thought that we'd all know exactly when the children were coming, and had wondered why not one of us had ever sent a note or even a packet of Barry's tea.

'Do you still go out to the Trocadero?' she asked.

'No,' I lied, and can't to this day figure out why. (I didn't admit the lie to the others.)

'She's staying there, I presume,' Caitriona said, lacing the words with flatness so they could suggest either sorrow or relief.

'She didn't say,' I replied.

'Ah, here come the Sambucas.'

TELLING

A very good Irish writer was giving a workshop to a group of fledgling writers, all women. He was one of the best. There are twelve bests. Lucky, M thought, four of those twelve are women. Unluckily (because at that time she thought that it was mere luck and not subterfuge which decided these matters), no one else knew that four of the twelve are women. She was glad to be in the same room as this man, not because she thought that she could learn anything from him, and this, not because he had nothing to teach, but because she didn't want to learn what he knew, she was on a slip road from that sort of thing, a hill that would get a better view. Still, she was glad, because his act of speaking to them, even if it was an uncomfortable faraway act, showed a humility that surprised her in one so great.

There were eight others in the room besides M: one who hoped to write a novel, three short-story people, already in love with the hurtful intimacy of that form, two possible poets, one poet, and one who wished to be a playwright (she hadn't a hope – that is, if getting a play performed is an essential part of being a playwright). There may have been others too, but M can't remember them. One of the short-story devotees was a lesbian, an honest, carefree person, who saw things that the others couldn't hear, and who ran a women's disco every Thursday night. The great writer spent a lot of time asking her questions. She answered as if she knew what he was up to. He didn't pass too much remarks on M, because her desired place of parking made her virtually invisible. The poets had their work cut out for them, even paying attention was hard, and who knows yet if the novelist was prepared to make her task a way of life, if she would ever be able to produce anything greater than a tome of lists or brand names. After lunch the sun shone, in that contradictory way that it suddenly can in Ireland, and because they were already tired from trying to justify their existences to themselves and to each other over lunch, a lethargy descended upon them, an itchiness could be noticed in some legs. Then the writer told them a story. And told them how to write it.

A man and woman in the west of Ireland were married. They had two children. The man was rarely home, because in the summer he spent his time with tourists, showing them this and that, being a great fellow altogether. The tourists thought that he was the salt of the earth and would remember him at odd moments in the middle of England or on an autobahn, for a month or so after their holidays. In the winter he did a little work on his small raggedy farm, but spent most of his time in the pub, where things were more jovial than at home. It was dark in the pub, but it was dark everywhere else too. The closing lights and the Guinness made him sullen and, certainly, going home made him even crosser. What happened behind the door when he closed it after him each night no one knew, because although the roads around were littered with signs proclaiming that this was a Neighbourhood Watch area, this did not mean that people watched their neighbours. If a stranger came and battered a woman, that would be serious, but what a local did in his own house was his own business. And something untoward was going on.

When the children reached an age when they could be shooshed away from her legs without danger, the woman got a part-time job in the post office. She loved it, the contact with every single person lit her up inside, making her remember a little of what used to be her hopes, none of them outlandish, all of them concerned with a quiet decent life with an adequate man who would give her the odd laugh and who would love her, without necessarily going on about it. The post office was the best place, because here she saw the steady saving in small books and how easy it was to hand over a few pounds, how worth it it was to see the numbers climbing up and up. From the very first week she put part of her wages into a savings account, from the first week was the best way, there would be no great flourish of buying followed by a suspicious drop. She could have been an adviser to bank robbers. As her children grew, fed by the pourings of an invisible, but still active, umbilical cord, so too did her nest egg. Two tourist summers and three unbearable winters later, the money was tangible, not much, but it would pay rent for some shabby aching flat that would have three inadequate single beds in it, one for herself and one each for her children when they would visit. Yes visit, because she couldn't afford to take them away. Yet.

When the spring came in she left. Her children too. For the moment. Just until she could afford to move them in with her into a place that would not lose out so badly in comparison to their own bungalow. Her first name was Hope. She left, her children too, because what was happening in the hallway of her home, with the lights out, was truly untoward, and the light was kept broken in there all the time. No matter how often she fixed it. The bulb disappeared or the switch was mysteriously broken or the socket had a chip out of it.

In a matter of months the husband allowed her back into the

bungalow in the afternoons. That way she could be there when the children came home from school. And maybe she'd put on a bit of tea for him while she was hanging about doing nothing. The joy of seeing them each evening burst out of her, making her skin flush and her hair gleam. Of course, she saw them every morning too, she turned up outside the school with extra foosies for their lunch. It was easy, the school only being one mile off the road that led from the flat to the post office. Her savings should have been dwindling fast but somehow she managed to put a finger in the dyke. Yet it would never be enough. And the law was not on her side.

Surprise was the first reaction when a legacy arrived from a cold, tight aunt, one who knew very well exactly what her niece was up to, and who changed her will in the last week of her life. Who could have thought that such anarchy played in the heart of one so buttoned up? The surprise was followed by the more appropriate reaction, an overwhelming, blushing feeling of being a winner, a warmth in the stomach as sure as if coming from an eternal flame lit behind the belly button. The woman began to lay her plans carefully, secretly; she spoke to her children with a boiling lightness in her voice. Her husband must not know.

But the town was small and word of her luck leaked out. Unknown to her, her husband did find out. It was on a Thursday, this in what was to be her last week before escape, that she was baking bread in the bungalow, her back to the door, answering homework questions on addition, subtraction and wars, when her husband came in. He ordered the children to leave and because children do not always know how to do the right thing, they did. She was putting raisins in the brown bread when she turned to face him, closing one hand on the mixture.

'If you go out that door again,' he said, 'I'll kill you.'

The woman knew that he meant it. He must not have expected disobedience, because as she moved to the door he thought that she was only changing her place in the room. But she bolted out, making a run for it like a woman possessed. He got his gun, the one he used when shooting with tourists, took aim and shot her once through the back of the head. When people reached her, the wheaten meal and the raisins were still in her hand.

The great writer swallowed. 'It's a true story,' he said, 'and you can use it, I don't want it. Your story is in the wheaten meal and raisins.'

M and the rest stared at him, a kind of communal choking smothering their voices. Their rage was too thick to be spread out for examination.

'End of session,' he said brightly, leaving the room, already oblivious of all those pairs of eyes.

The story, of course, was not in the raisins, it was in him telling the tale to a room full of women and thinking that it was. Or more than the story, the wonder is that a few of them, the poets perhaps, didn't cry, or that one of them, the novelist maybe, didn't attack him with a brush that the hopeful playwright, being already used to the notion of props, would have just happened to have had handy. But neither is that the story. It is rather what the fledgling writers thought of what the great man said. But no, it may not be that either, it may be instead what you think of what they thought of what he thought.

THE SOUND OF TWIN

When we were young I know that people tended to like me more than they did my brother. I was quiet, a thing people like in a child, and I learned to play on that. I also picked up manners easily and never tired practising them.

'Now what would you like Damien?'

'Bread and jam, please,' I'd say, if that's what was on the table.

'And Darragh, I suppose you'll want something different?'

Sometimes Darragh would force himself to say, 'The same thing, the same thing', but I could tell that it was killing him. He was bursting to be different.

'Are you sure?' they'd ask him, never letting him be, needling him into being difficult.

I felt sorry for my brother but couldn't help it if I was better liked. Loved in fact. We were twins, are twins. Identical. But only in looks. By the time we were nine years old people tuned to the trappings of civility could tell us apart because of our manners. I cultivated a voice that went smartly with my obsequiousness. In contrast, Darragh's accent roughened and toughened.

In the playground, when boys started to fight with me, by mistake, Darragh always came running and they scattered, either to leave us completely to our own devices or to return suddenly, as if they had forgotten something serious, to get stuck into him, with a particular viciousness, because they hated the mistake of mixing us up. Darragh learned to fight really well. If they left us alone, he would stay with me for a few moments before scarpering off to his important business of football. I had said the word before he did, but that's as far as my expertise shone. If I had rescued him the way he saved me, I would surely have said, Are you all right now? But Darragh never said a word.

I remember myriads of incidents from our childhoods. But they don't seem important to me. I can call them up, as you would a file, to check proofs of things that I have just thought. Yes, that's Darragh, that fits in with such and such a day. I knew that my childhood was merely a waiting room. From the day that I sat in low infants, making words with my chalk, and learning to respond properly to praise, I knew that there was something waiting for me.

We grew at the same rate. Even our teeth were the same. Our mother did her best. She dressed us in similar clothing, but not exactly the same. I think she got discounts in draper's shops because of the twin element in the transaction, but she would add some little flourish to the new clothes to differentiate between us – change the buttons, sew an extra pocket on a shirt, that sort of thing. But it made no difference, people still mixed us up; no one noticed her endeavours except herself. And me. Although, as the days after purchase and alteration moved on, I too forgot.

I was better at school than my brother, although it was hard for the teachers to tell. They had to put us at the furthest ends of rooms, or sometimes, that having failed, beside each other, where they would stare at us for a few moments. I knew what they were at, sinking in some formula that they had just worked out to tell us apart. My proficiency at lessons went with my general demeanour. Even if I'd wanted to, I would never have had the nerve not to do my best. Darragh, on the other hand, developed different skills – copying, bluffing and lying. In later years, due to these skills, girls left him after a few months because they discovered that he was not the person they had thought he was. With me they got no surprises. At school I did what I was told to do. Of course, I didn't relish doing what didn't suit me, I'm not a complete dodo, but I did it anyway. Darragh, never. How I envied him. And he thought ahead. He asked me what subjects I had chosen for the Leaving Certificate. 'Right then, I'll do three the same and three different. You can do my last three exams.'

He had even worked out the timetable so that the examination time of his last three subjects would not clash with mine. It never occurred to me to argue, it seemed a little enough thing to do for all that saving from all those kicks and thumps on the face. And there was no risk attached – unless they fingerprinted us on the day, no one would know the difference between us. By now our acne, which had appeared in almost symmetrical spottiness, was gone. In the school holidays we had tried beards, but the same streak of squiggly red had appeared in each one. Even Darragh thought this too ridiculous.

Darragh did better in his Leaving Certificate than he should have. We did not take the same subjects when we went to university. More Leaving Certificate strategy. It is because of this that I know the degrees of knowing something. I know that just because a person appears to know something does not mean that they do. The girls still left him after a few months. But he did begin to learn things, not from books, and not deep down, he was too busy for that, but surface things that would get him by.

We got our holiday jobs. I got shifts at a newspaper and

Darragh delivered post. I believe that this is when our ways geared themselves up for real parting. I became involved in the serious matters of news, the ins and outs of how decisions taken thousands of miles away come home to roost, the historical patterns of our lives, the similarities of divergent cultures. Darragh became allied with the bits and pieces of the letters he delivered, the things that people think are news, bills, aunts dying, babies being born, Dear Johns, football results. The link broke. How could I possibly, particularly now that I could see a serious future before me, care less about the foibles of lives that were just going to repeat patterns ad nauseam, day by day, year by year? No, I was not going to be suffocated by trivia.

I did become even more solicitous of Darragh, because if I hadn't, the truth might have rolled out and drowned us. There was one last thing, in our final year, that saved us. We played the part of Gar in *Philadelphia, Here I Come!* Audiences flocked to see it because of our likeness, it gave new life to the play. People understood split personalities by looking at us, the curling of my lip, our lips, made people aware of the viciousness of secrecy. Our production won every medal going. Directors would be reluctant to put it on again for a number of years, until they could get the picture of us out of their heads. The author slipped in one night and apparently left mesmerised, not having known until then what he had written. At the end of each evening's performance even our separate friends mixed in pubs. It was harder on mine than his.

We got away from each other not a moment too soon. I learned to breathe properly, not in shallow gasps. It seems to me that the break could have been, and should have been, equally beneficial for Darragh. But he chose to squander it and became even more deeply dug into the frivolities of life. He tried to keep in touch with me, but as I travelled the world and the world of minds I really had no interest. I was still meticulously polite in our telephone conversations, I could always tidy my desk while he spoke. Rabbited on. By then I was a war correspondent, which was, of course, incongruous if one considered the school yard. Darragh was a salesman. He got as excited about his gadgets as I got about retreating armies. He showed his excitement; I didn't show mine.

During the six months that I spent in the Near East I did not speak to Darragh at all. I sent one postcard explaining the impossibility of communication, even postal. I didn't want a reply, because our writing looks exactly the same. I wanted no reminders. I didn't want to get envelopes that looked as if they were self-addressed. I relished the lack of phone calls, the absence of intrusion. There was no one to talk of resemblances, so I began to develop an image of my own. I lightened up a little, which is not the easiest thing to do when one's work involves body counts. By the time my Christmas visit began to approach I had built a whole persona for myself.

I arrived in Dublin airport amidst the ferocious buzzing of islanders returning home. I was as pleased as anyone else, although the war job had added an extra wariness to me, other, that is, than the one which I had deliberately refined. I met Darragh for drinks in a pub. I fell in with the general excitement of the season and thought that perhaps a new, appropriate phase of our adulthood had arrived. But he insisted that we meet again the following evening and, despite my reservations, I agreed.

It was a disaster of a night. There were some old mates there, still belonging to him. He jumped from conversation to conversation, pronouncing widely on everything, loudest on that about which he knew nothing. He told endless stories about past things that I had purposely forgotten. He and the mates seemed to relish my discomfort. It proved that they had dragged me down a peg or two. I began to hate his voice and to worry that I too might sound like him. Surely not possible. This will never happen again, I swore to myself in the toilet, the only place I managed to grab back bits of my life. The holiday stretched interminably in front of me. I have no idea how I put up with him, them all. The gadgets, the stories. In order to escape early, I invented a resurgence of the war without a trace of guilt or worry about being caught. There was no fear that they would check. I saw something in Darragh's eyes but looked away quickly. By the time I got to the airport I wasn't sure if I liked myself. But the check-in restored my confidence.

In the five years that followed some normal semblance of sibling civility was established. On my travels I even spoke about my twinhood sometimes, my view of it, naturally. I didn't mix with the sort of people who might question my analysis. We had more serious matters to discuss. My dreams were usually clear. And, as had always been the way, I had no trouble meeting women. Enough to keep me going. We were in a fleeting world: they took their pleasure, I took mine. Then I met a particular woman, an Irishwoman. In truth I would have preferred a woman of different nationality but we cannot control everything, I suppose. She was an aid worker on leave. She threw herself into the holiday as aid workers will. They carouse in direct contrast to the horrors they have seen. I was fascinated by her. The shape of her, the movement of her, the Cork sound of her, the electricity in her hair, the whole look of her. She told me that she was in love with me too. But on her fourth visit she dropped me. Said I was too serious, that she couldn't knock out fun with me any more. I believe that she enjoyed the journey to places better than the arrival. I told her as much and she said, 'See what I mean?'

Whatever that woman did to me my luck changed with others. Perhaps I got hesitant, perhaps they smelt fear and failure from me, I don't know, but my luck certainly altered.

It had to be luck because my manner was the same, as was my outward appearance, more or less. The more I was refused, the more I was refused. Despite my better judgement, I listened to love songs on the radio to see if they'd give me any clues. Not a chance. It would have been good to speak to somebody, but what would I say? A heaviness worked its way down my body from my shoulders to the flats of my feet.

Then a letter arrived, unexpectedly announcing Darragh's engagement. I'm the person who thought it was unexpected. It was because of my own woman trouble that it startled me. Him! Him who was always being left. Not any more, it seemed. And here was I making comparisons between us! They were having an engagement party, just a bit of a thing, nothing very formal, a few drinks really, that was all, and they, himself and Maighread, would be delighted if I could make it. There was no need to let them know if I couldn't. Somehow he had managed to make the informality of the few drinks very formal indeed. I bet that woman had been talking to him and now he would have a completely different take on me. Well, I would be there, by God I would. And they wouldn't know a thing about it until I turned up. Surprise as weapon. Surprise as disruption mechanism of weekend plans.

I arrived in Dublin the night before the drinks. It was an interesting thing to do, to re-enter one's own country unannounced. It felt like slipping through the back door. I checked into a hotel – again, an interesting thing to do in one's own city. I had a great desire to be bossy at the reception desk. This came from the relief of knowing tones of voices, the fact that I wouldn't be letting my country down if I was unmannerly. It was my country. Darragh would have laughed at me. There he was again, Darragh, Darragh, Darragh.

I went to a nightclub. And my luck changed. Marion was a nice woman, may indeed have been a lovely woman, for all I know. I was too preoccupied with relief to engage in normal noticing. She came to my hotel bedroom easily, as is the way these days, as has in fact been the way for a long time. Hotel managers of the sixties didn't get those nosy eyes out of the blue nor overnight. And our night together was a lot more than competent. Abstinence had made me careful and appreciative. She had to leave, but would meet me tomorrow evening. I had decided to bring her along with me to the informal formal. Arrive unannounced and with a woman as usual. She dithered a little, having apparently had a previous sort of arrangement, but then decided that she could cancel it. That was a good sign for my luck.

When Marion and I met the following evening we were discreet in our pleasure at seeing each other afresh. As we arrived at the door she said, 'That's funny', but I was too busy preening myself for the effect of my arrival and taming my vindictiveness to notice the hesitancy in her voice. I ushered her in and pranced proudly two inches behind. In the three seconds that it took for the scene to register itself on me, Darragh and his fiancée had unfortunately turned around to face me. There he was, my double, with his arm draped confidently over the bare shoulders of his wife-to-be, a woman bearing every single physical feature of my date. There must have been some silence, then the women erupted into uproarious laughter.

My brother recovered his jauntiness and said, 'Good God, what a surprise, brother mine.'

Brother mine! Where had he found such an absurd expression?

Some fool, who obviously had not seen Marion yet, hollered, 'Great to see Damien and Darragh together.'

Damien and Darragh. Our names rolled off his tongue together as if we were the same breath of air. My face boiled

over. The heat spread down my chest much in the way I expect the menopause travels on the skins of women. My head
bobbed lightly on my shoulders, making me look, no doubt,
like an ornamental dog in a moving car. My saliva seemed to
have disappeared, one of my knees began to twitch, I wished
that the other one would also contract so that I could have
some sense of balance. And still the women laughed. Now
Darragh joined them. And, as others realised what had happened, they added guffaws and giggles and baritonal snorts,
until a landslide of mirth and hilarity flooded the room. The
noise was overwhelming.

As Darragh moved towards me I could think of only one
thing, how to get out of there. Easy, lift one foot and put it in
front of the other. My desire for escape pumped into the far-
thest reaches of every sinew in my body. It was not just because
of embarrassment that I wanted to leave, it was also because I
was afraid that the murder I felt might be seen in my eyes. But
Darragh was only two feet away from me, one foot, six inches,
and he threw his arms around me in the most overdone rugbic
crush I have ever felt. I was trapped, lost, with no war to save
me. There was nothing for it but to stay, pass the night in beer
time, call up the reserves of manners that I had assiduously performed since being a young boy. It may have been the worst
night of my life.

That was two years ago. For obvious reasons I didn't go to
the wedding, Marion was bridesmaid. I'm thinking of them
tonight, here in Kosovo, because I've just had a letter telling
me that Maighread was safely delivered of identical twin boys
on the first of April. So here it is, that thing that was waiting
for me. May God help the one who is most like me.

THE PARK

Apparently my blood pressure is the same as everyone else's, that is, just below boiling point. The fat which, during the last few years, had wrapped itself like a tight hug around my arse, has begun to disappear. Where does fat go when it falls off people? Are there chunks of it floating around the air in the exact spot where people have got thin, and where is the exact spot, and do people breathe it in and does it damage their lungs? My nerves are no worse than they ever were, and I sleep well. These things surprise me but they don't surprise Brigid. Nothing surprises her, that's why I love her, and her eyes are grey.

Brigid was going through a bad time, doing her best to get through each day without making an ass of herself. Her boy-friend (she would call him a lover, because she has confidence like that) was away. Again. But this time there was an eeriness about his absence, an insistence, that seemed to be trying to tell her something. She was finding it difficult to put her days in, days based on promises, particularly since, as she had begun to admit to herself, the promises had never actually been put into words and said. She had a notch up from a middling job in the corporation and the sort of car that a woman like her can afford in a country which, eleven years later, was to miss the point completely and interview the staple diet of men on the night that Mary Robinson was elected president. She was driving home in this car wondering, and trying not to, if there would be a letter from him when she got there. More of those flags had appeared. This area had been coming down with flags for the past week. New ones sprouted every evening as if there had been multiple births all day long when people who had work were at it. A local festival she presumed, a very spready local festival by the looks of it.

There was a long letter from him that said nothing but wished she was there, which was something. She bit the inside of her lip, wondering again, until it bled. She walked around her flat in a disarrayed fashion, picking things up and putting them down somewhere else. Sheena rang her and asked her if they wanted to go out to dinner tonight.

'It's for Macartan McElwaine, he's emigrating next week, lucky divil.'

'There's no we, only me,' she said.

'Ah, is Diarmuid away again? Well, come yourself.'

Because something is better than nothing, she went. She took the poor-route bus into town, the quickest journey, the one that makes no effort to avoid the desolate patches. She tried not to hear the tightly packed sounds of poverty. Not tonight.

'Your perm's still in.'

'It'd need to be. I only got it done a month next Thursday.'

The restaurant was perfect. It could dismiss the outside world in a matter of seconds. It had the right consistency – ordinary enough to be relaxing, slightly exotic, so Brigid could be interested, a little conservative, so she could count herself exotic in contrast. This hanging between realities made her dizzy with satisfaction.

The others came together. There was Jacinta, a long-term

student who always had money from somewhere and who was more used to spending it in pubs than in restaurants; Sheena, an indifferent clerk in the Norwich Union Insurance Corporation, a dedicated northerner whose mind was sharp as razors; Macartan, dreamy and absent always, but even more so tonight because he was already drinking fast drinks in Manhattan; and Padhraig Copeland, whose father, a Connemara *Gaeilgeoir*, had married a Basque woman, who sometimes spoke Spanish with an overlay of longing.

They fussed and hugged and sat down and ordered wine and made plenty of noise. They were of the runaway generation. Brigid too. There were no family heirlooms, even cheap ones, in their sitting rooms, because none of them had been forgiven, not yet anyway. Perhaps later they would be, when the death of a parent might force reconciliations on the one left behind. As teenagers they had bitten and sniggered at everything, and when they got to be twenty they didn't have to swallow their words because things were better then.

Brigid liked staring at people. She was mesmerised by their hair, their faces, their clothes. She could see sloppy sewing through an overcoat. Looking at these people, what could she see? Jacinta never had to seek first attention because she had carrot-magenta hair. Since the sixties, when it was first allowed that red could be matched with pink, or other reds, or any colour, Jacinta had started wearing shocking blood lipstick. She wore it still, even though the time had not yet come around again when thinking women could paint themselves. Padhraig Copeland was far too good-looking – there should be a law against anyone having such a perfect face and mouth. No one ever noticed what he was wearing. Macartan McElwaine had a startled face, a crooked nose, and hair so straight it looked wet. Sheena was so puny she nearly had no face at all; therefore her voice came always as a surprise, a big deep thing that had its way perfectly curved around difficult ideas. She had fed her intelligence well. Brigid would have a good night after all.

Sheena was concerned about the impending visit of the pope to Ireland. 'It will knock us back years,' she said.

So that's what all the flags were for. Brigid wondered to herself where the people had got them. Had they had them all the time in boxes, away with the Christmas decorations, waiting in case the pope ever did come to Ireland? Or was there a factory somewhere spewing them out of machines at a rate of knots? Or did the women sew them up at night in their individual homes and pretend that they had had them all along?

'Look how much damage he particularly of all the popes has done, in how many years? How long has he been pope now?'

Jacinta remembered. Exactly. Because she was picked out of a crowd on the night of a Reclaim the Night march in Dublin by a TV personality and asked if she would come on his programme and say how she could defend not letting men go on the march in support of the women's demand that they should be able to walk safely down the streets at any time, day or night, without men. Well, that's not the way the TV personality put it. She said yes. When she got there her knees were knocking together with fright and she had forgotten that television was in colour so her clothes were all wrong (how could she have thought that, her and her shocking blood lipstick?). But she was saved, because the first Polish pope ever had just been chosen and *Today Tonight* had spent all evening scouring Dublin for a Polish priest. By the time they got one, all the Polish priests were paralytic on vodka. So there he was, his English not the best in the first place, slurring his way through his interview. In comparison to him, Jacinta sounded like a professional.

Sheena was so concerned at the assumption that we all wanted the pope here she said that something should be done about it. '*We* should do something,' she said.

And that led to a long discussion about what they would do, what they couldn't do, what they could do and what they dared to do.

And so by the end of the meal they had decided to paint slogans, so that people would know there was some opposition in the country. They believed that to be important. Nothing too drastic like 'Fuck the Pope', because that could be taken up the wrong way, twice. Nothing too obscure, because people would just knit their eyebrows and not understand. Something simple like 'No Priest State Here'. They would do it on the road from Maynooth to Dublin.

'Maynooth,' Macartan said dreamily, turning it on his tongue as a child would repeat a word to itself, knowing that it meant something but not knowing what. 'Maynooth, where priests are made.'

Brigid was given the job of driving down and up to Maynooth once or twice over the next few days to calculate how many special branch cars were cruising the route. 'Branch cars! How will I know them?'

'You'll feel them on the back of your neck,' Sheena said.

During the week, Brigid dreamt that she was a bird flying into people's kitchens, into canteens, on to building sites, switching the bloody radios off as they built up cosy pictures of the wonderful preparations for the wonderful man, the way a radio voice can.

The night came, the night before he was to come. Brigid felt nervous in an alert way, pleased that they were doing at least some little thing. She had plenty of petrol, oil and water in the car. She had cleaned it while she was at it. The tins of paint were in the boot. She was clean herself, spruced up in a pair of jeans that had zips where no zips where needed, a royal blue, light jumper, a white shirt collar peeping up around the neck.

They had decided to leave her flat after midnight. The later they painted the slogans, the more chance they would remain unnoticed until morning, when people would see them on their way to work and be outraged or smile gleefully with relief. It was a long evening. At twelve o'clock or thereabouts Sheena and Macartan arrived. By half past twelve it was obvious that Jacinta and Padhraig had had second thoughts and were not in favour of pursuing a wildcat decision taken in a restaurant when there had been plenty of wine drunk, all because Macartan was emigrating – oh yes! leaving the place, but brave enough to do one last thing for the oul' sod before he abandoned it altogether, easy for him. And as for Sheena, she'd think better of it when she remembered her job; and as for Brigid, she'd never.

So Macartan, Sheena and Brigid set out and drove through the early autumn night. Sometimes they checked to see if Brigid's calculations of the branch cars were correct – every eight minutes, every five minutes, that's not one, oh, it is, it is, I can feel it – but mostly they behaved as if they were out on a mid-afternoon Sunday drive.

The first one was the hardest. They reached the spot that Brigid had picked out before they had decided who would do it. They shouted at each other and jumped around in their seats as if a flea had bitten them. But they calmed down and decided that Sheena and Macartan would do the first ones in rota while Brigid sat at the wheel and started the car up again when they got to the second last E. If they were getting on well, she could have a go when they got to a quieter spot.

OK, here goes. NO PRIEST STATE HERE in luminous white paint, lucid in the dark, as if it had been there for all time. They had to tear themselves away. They could have stood around for hours chatting, taking the odd, long, admiring look at it, remarking on how well the letters were done, smelling the paint, watching the moon watching it. The second one, a mile from Maynooth, lacked originality, didn't look as pleasing, but maybe that was because of the bad background wall, which didn't show the letters up terribly well. The straight stretch of characterless road took away from it too. Still, it was done. And a third. By now the rhythm was flawless – they had the paint and brush and painters out and in again in one minute.

They were concentrating so hard on the fourth, enjoying themselves so much, making the letters flourish more, that they didn't hear the car coming until it had rounded the corner ahead of them. Quick as a flash, Brigid switched on the engine and moved forward. The driver would think he had only imagined that the car had been stopped. Macartan and Sheena jumped across the hedge, scratching their legs on thorns. Sheena got stung by a nettle. They sat in the ditch listening to their hearts drumming one long beat in their ears. Brigid drove around the corner, switched off the engine, listened, and when no sound came, she reversed back to the spot. While the two were extricating themselves from the ditch and getting into the car, Brigid, bold as brass, finished off the HERE.

'Phew! If that had happened with our first one, we would have scarpered home.'

Because of the fright, they turned left at Lucan and took the Strawberry Beds road. 'Just as good for commuters in the morning and far safer for this business and more beautiful anyway,' they consoled each other with something near love, born from the fear, that was rising up in their voices. They looked at the road, its tall trees crowded together in places, gossiping, its houses perched dangerously on the edge of steep hills, leaning over to hear. Brigid's mother had walked dogs along this road once, when she worked as a doctor's housekeeper. The dogs were well fed. Had Brigid's mother ever wondered at the beauty? Was she asleep at this moment, having a peculiar dream about the time she worked in Dublin for that doctor?

The drive was so pleasant it was hard to remember that they had stops to make. Did Brigid's car stop at the very places where her mother had taken a rest with the dogs, listened to the river whispering and making music? Who knows? She couldn't quite remember how many they had done on the Beds road, five at least – she had got to do two herself. The one that stretched across the road, that's the one she liked best, it was under a thick black tree and the RE ran into the roadside, staining the grass as it broke up. It was that grass you can whistle on if you cup it properly between your hand and lips.

They drove homewards, talking louder now, laughing a lot at nothing, relief beginning to take them over. They drove up Oxmantown Road, down the North Circular, left at Phibsboro, getting further away, getting nearer a door they could close behind them.

For some reason, they couldn't let it go, this night-time artistry, they stopped to do one last one opposite the gates of Glasnevin Cemetery. Funny, that was the one that stayed the longest. A Garda car passed them as they drove off.

'Shit, we nearly got caught,' Macartan said.

'Nearly pregnant never did anyone any harm,' Sheena said.

When they got to Brigid's flat they were ravenous. Macartan and Sheena checked the car for stray splashes of paint, then washed the brushes. Brigid made fried egg, tomato and mushrooms on toast. Macartan stayed the night.

In the morning they switched stations on the radio. One news bulletin mentioned that some vandals had daubed a protest slogan against the pope's visit.

'*A* slogan, only *one*, is that so?' Brigid said sleepily as she fiddled with the tuner. 'The pope this, the pope that, and the pope the other,' she muttered and switched it off.

By the time they got up, the country was in full swing, children bathed and dressed already, if they were travelling far to the park, cars washed, minds battened down, bus tickets secured and picnics packed. People who lived in the city were out buying their plastic chairs. Hawkers were converging on the park. The last stones of the park's inconvenient walls were being tipped into the dump – they had to go to make room for all the cars, guards, priests, mothers, bankers, a few radicals who had decided to make a fortune selling periscopes, councillors, fathers, poets, and musicians who had finely tuned themselves to receive the Body and Blood of Jesus Christ. Those who thought otherwise, were, simply, invisible for the day. By nine o'clock in the morning no amount of floodlights could have picked them out. (It took a certain kind of flash violence to make so many disappear. There are bruises left. There are sounds of strangling. But there you go . . . choking sounds, well, that's only to be expected, it couldn't be avoided . . .)

Brigid's doorbell rang. She went to it slowly because she was feeling the effects of erasure, and the small gurgling of anger in the pit of her stomach was not enough antidote. She opened the door to her smiling brother and his careful girlfriend, her cousins and their friends. They had come early so as to get a good view and to buy some of those chairs if there were any left and they would park their cars here if she didn't mind.

'We thought we'd get our tea here as I'm sure there's no place open,' her brother said, moving into the hallway.

Brigid felt as if they would crush her if she didn't step aside. She backed into the kitchen. The last one closed the door behind him. They were standing now around Diarmuid's packed luggage. She hated them doing that. That was all she had of him – as long as his belongings were packed in boxes here, here in her room, there was hope. If these pope visitors hung around his things for long, he might never come back. Look at that big ignorant mouth leaning his dirty arse on Diarmuid's stereo. Now that she had woken a little, flashes of anger were skittering through her, shaking her up and strengthening her legs.

She said, 'I'm not making tea for anyone on their way to see the pope.'

They all laughed.

'I'm not,' she said.

They laughed again.

'No really,' she said, as the laugh petered out.

Her brother said, 'You were always great crack. I was just saying that recently. We miss your crack in Mullingar, we could be doing with it especially on a Monday morning. Right, who wants tea, who wants coffee?'

Brigid went to the door, opened it, and said, 'I'm serious. No one on their way to the park is welcome here. The whole country is at your disposal today, so why are you bothering me? I'll have enough trouble all day keeping that creep out of my mind without having to feed his followers on their way . . . Enough said, I won't insult you, just get your tea and your posters and your rosary beads somewhere else.'

They did leave. Well, what else could they do? Their hearts winced at the only blow struck against a believer that day. How well it had to be them! Brigid couldn't believe they had actually gone. The triumph left no taste of ashes in her mouth. She said 'Whoopee' and went back to bed with Macartan, where she curled her bare body as close to his as possible, merging her chest into his so their hearts might beat together. He wasn't Diarmuid but he was here.

A few hours later they heard a cheer go up from the street.

Her neighbours were all hanging out upstairs windows, waving yellow and white flags at a speck in the sky that must be your man's helicopter. Brigid lifted the nearest black garment to hand, which happened to be a nightdress, attached it firmly to her window, and got back into bed again, trying to shut out the noises of belligerent piety.

At half past eleven she and Macartan decided to go to Newgrange, the most pagan place they could think of. They drove alone along roads that wove through north County Dublin townlands, roads that skirted the pope's intended route to Drogheda, meeting the odd branch car, the occupants of which pinned eyes on them – what could those two people be doing? Where could they possibly be going? Mass was on in the park by now, wasn't it? The pope had already told the people in icy sharp tones what they must not do, and nor must you, and you must not, and also . . .

It would take the people years to recover from the things being said in such a way on such a day. As a million and more genuflected, creaking their knees within a quarter of a second of each other, Macartan put his feet up on the dashboard and sighed the way some of us do when making love has satisfied us beyond what we think we deserve. The pope raised the host, the people bowed their heads, Brigid wondered if that was her period starting now. The people filed in straight lines to get communion, some shuffling, some stamping, as they edged their way confidently towards heaven. Brigid shivered in a flash of cold.

People had started opening their flasks in the park by the time Macartan and Brigid reached the gate. CLOSED DUE TO THE POPE'S VISIT. They said nothing, just caught each other's hands tight and started looking for an opening in the hedge. They climbed through a slit in the ditch and jumped onto the hard ground. Macartan felt as if his hip bones had been pushed up to his ribs with the impact.

The people sang and swayed: 'He's got the whole world in his hands.' (Eleven years later, when some of the poison was leaving, a few people sang 'She's got the whole world in her hands' to Mary Robinson as she drove through the park gates. They giggled low down, knowing where they'd heard it last.) Macartan and Brigid reached the stone wall. Brigid caught Macartan's face and stuck her tongue down his throat. Across the city they had just left, odd souls longed for the comfort of a warm body, the big crook of an arm to bury their faces in, a chest to lie on, a mouth to kiss, anything to take their minds off it.

Brigid and Macartan went into town that night to have a drink. It was the worst thing they could have done for their hearts, because they met too many people who had gone to the park, people they expected more from, were surprised at, and there was a strange sound or was it a smell lurking in the shadows. The streets were full of rubbish, as if an army had trampled through today and left a wash after it. If that was so, Brigid and Macartan were swimming precariously on the edge of it, being watched by the backs of the people on deck. They met Padhraig and Jacinta, who were now furious with themselves for not having gone painting. They had spent the day sitting on a bed together, but they didn't get into it because Padhraig was gay, much to Jacinta's disappointment, not always, but on this day! They waved home-made flags at the screen and shouted, 'Up the pole. Up the pole.'

They all had a drink. The four of them whispered together, hoping to draw some consolation from each other, but it didn't feel enough.

At the airport, Sheena, Brigid, Padhraig and Jacinta hung around while Macartan's parents went through the emotions. Macartan's mother was furious with grief. She would wait six months or more before sending him postcards of the west, of pubs in the west, of musical instruments under blue skies, of valleys pinpointed by intimate rivers and lakes in the west. She would wait. Brigid couldn't kiss him properly, his parents didn't turn their heads for long enough. In the toilet Sheena and Brigid decided to go out together painting once more. Why? There was no need. It must have been the airport, the sense of people fleeing. It must have been. They didn't tell Padhraig or Jacinta – it was too serious.

They drove to the park in the early darkness and painted IF MEN GOT PREGNANT CONTRACEPTION AND ABORTION WOULD BE SACRAMENTS on the monument built for the pope's visit. There were lots of letters. Brigid did fifty of them, hers looked sudden and fluid. Sheena's seven were non-runny and perfect. In the paper the next day you could tell there had been two people. The worst part of it all was doing what Sheena said they had to do afterwards – go to the nearest pub, pee on their hands, and then wash them under the tap. The worst, but she was right. It got rid of the paint from around their fingernails. Sheena then told Brigid that she, too, was emigrating. Brigid said, 'Aw God no', missing her like death already.

Brigid got caught painting a harmless slogan seven years later, one year after the passing of the statute of limitations.

'It may be a harmless slogan, your honour, but the vandalism of the papal cross in the park wasn't.'

The judge's eyes widened into white. 'Six months,' he said.

I got caught. I had a standby job taking in the lottery ticket money in my local shop any time the lottery reached seven hundred thousand pounds or more. A customer left half the receipt one night. The winning numbers were marked on it. Not knowing (I should have) which receipt was needed to claim a prize, I chanced my arm and brought the docket in.

By an odd coincidence a hundred pounds went missing from the till the same week. Not me, I wouldn't have the nerve.

'A hundred pounds may not be a lot of money, your honour, but attempting to procure fraudulently eight hundred and sixty thousand, two hundred and ninety-two pounds is.'

'Six months,' he said.

We're getting out next week and Diarmuid is throwing a party for us.

TAKING SCARLET
AS A REAL COLOUR
OR AND ALSO, SUSAN . . .

I'll tell you what it says in books, Susan. I never wanted to read and I wish I'd never started, but that's like an alcoholic moaning about the Christmas pudding, it's too late now. Not that reading kills you. Physically. I'm delighted to be somewhere now. When people ask me, where were you the day Bonner saved the goal? I can tell them without shyness or shame. I know the exact spot. I was here in Dublin, one of my sister's children was sick, so we were watching it in the bedroom. We took turns putting our heads under the covers; it was my turn, so I had my head under the bedclothes during the actual second. I've seen the replay though. The night the Americans bombed Baghdad I was in a pub surrounded by citizens of the US of A. My luck, it was the only pub in Dublin where there was even one American. They were all there to hear the traditional music. The musicians stopped and stared at the TV with the rest of us, which was an odd thing to see, them doing the same thing as the rest of us. We could have tried to pretend that the sound of whizzing bombs was really a new-fangled synthesiser backing a tune but it wouldn't have worked. Everyone was pale, except some of the Americans.

There was no more music that night. Susan, where were you?
You go to bed very early, don't you? The day the pope came I
was in Cork. Do you remember that? Loads of people went to
Cork because it was a pope-free zone. Where were you, Susan?
No, don't tell me, I can guess. But the reason I started to read
was because I originally came from nowhere. When people ask
you where you were the day Kennedy was shot, I bet you can
tell them. Me? I was nowhere. Unless you'd call walking with
my sister up on the ditch down our road to the shop, carrying a
flashlamp that you had to shake all the time to get the battery
to connect with whatever it's supposed to connect with, the
frozen grass and weeds cutting patterns on our mucky welling-
tons, somewhere. Which I don't. The band – the bagpipe band
we called them as if we needed to differentiate between them
and all the other bands that we had, or maybe we just liked the
sound of 'bagpipe' – was practising in Gladys Mahaffey's
house, or, at least, it had been her house before she moved to
the village. Gladys was a prostitute; oh, yes, there are prosti-
tutes everywhere, even nowhere. She was a lovely woman,
kind, but unwise. She had rakes of children, all of them she
loved, Hickory Holler's Tramp wouldn't have been in it. The
children looked like the shopkeepers, the farmers, the labourers, the van drivers. We liked walking on the ditch because when we were sent to the shop, particularly at night,
my mother said, 'Don't walk on the ditch, you might fall into
the shuck.' And we shone the light, when it worked, all over
the sky, up and down from the tip of the earth to our welling-
ton boots, dancing over the Milky Way, teasing it as we
passed. It was probably the flashlight one of the band saw and
then came out to tell us that President John F. Kennedy was
shot. Killed stone dead. They must have had a wireless on all
the time, which would be odd because you couldn't hear it
over the drone of the practising bagpipers. It's more likely that

one of them was late and had just arrived with the news. Or maybe they had known it for a long time and saw us and thought that by the look of us we didn't know Kennedy was dead and felt that they'd better tell us. We were from nowhere, so he could have been dead for hours and we wouldn't have known. Around that time I started to read to lift the aching embarrassment of being no one from nowhere. Gladys had some kind of fit one night when a customer was with her, a Mr MacM. The word spread, so the men stopped turning up, but it was great for Gladys because they kept paying her, to keep her mouth shut, so she always had enough money to rear their children. Look at some of the women in this joint, Susan, I'm surprised that woman's finger doesn't go blue or fall off with the size of that ring, it's as colossal as a street lamp. Susan dear, it's not true that I wouldn't say that if I was married – I have longed for many impossible things in my life but married has never been one of them. When I was young I would have liked to have had polio. I reckoned it didn't kill you and you could have an attractive limp. I would have liked any kind of limp really, I told you I was from nowhere. In the end I was expected to settle for a bookless life of drib drabs, oh but no, they had me sized up wrong. Here, do you want a light? Did you know that every time you light a cigarette from a candle a sailor dies? I've sent shiploads perishing. I light a candle in the bathroom, put out the electricity and light a candle, very relaxing, and, of course, I've been to many expensive restaurants, where they always have candles. Some people would definitely say that I've done well, although I still think that a limp would have done me better, marked me out more clearly. But the books, Susan, I was talking about the books. I buried myself neck deep. I feasted, I swallowed, I took into me the way some people take vitamins. Imagine how I felt, I was somewhere. It was a long time later before it dawned on me that they were wrong about us. And that was a terrible thing. I still think of those books as the letters of a lover who turned out to be a fraud. What they didn't say about us is bad enough until you find out what they did say; yet, bad as that is, there is nothing worse than what they didn't say. A woman never had a baby in books, do you know that, Susan? Not once. There was an addition to a family, men ran up hospital stairs breathless to visit their wives who had just given them a child, there was a baby in the bed beside their wives where there hadn't been one before, or when a man died he had four children but a woman never had a child. There was none of that vomiting, no hysteria, no timid asking for him to support her back in the middle of the night, no ripping and tearing asunder, no screaming, no squelching around in blood, no enlarged vaginas. If we don't know what birth is like, we can conscript easier. That baby there, sucking milk, could become a war hero, Susan. So what? I say, anyone's ordinary boyfriend could become a hero, let's say, if next door went on fire and he rescued all the children or if he jumped into the Liffey to rescue an attempter of suicide – actually, I don't think that's heroic, I think that's interference – but you know what I mean. You don't have to kill someone to be a hero. All the interesting things, Susan, what a fraud. And another thing ... Stop getting your knickers in a knot, Susan, you're terribly easily embarrassed, aren't you? *And* you go to bed too early. No, I won't lower my voice, why should I? They never lower theirs. Come on, Susan, you remind me of a child I overheard yesterday saying to its mother, 'Mammy, don't I have manners?' You have manners all right, where will they get you? We need to know things. Unmannerly things. What we need to know I'll tell you in a minute. If I wrote a book, I'm not saying I would, that should be a relief, oh, smile, Susan, a joke never killed you yet. All the same, Sister Brigitta, an tSiúr Brigitta, always said that I

was good at English. She said it sadly, down in the bottom of
her boots, because she believed that if a girl was good at English, she couldn't be good at Irish. Poor Brigitta. I remember I
liked the way words could bring you somewhere. I was very
pleased to find out that 'hangar' meant a shed for housing aircraft. That meant that every time I thought of hangers, every
time I tidied the room, every Sunday morning when I got my
good coat out for mass, I travelled places on aircraft. At mass
my soul was in a state of grace, which meant that the hole underneath my heart was now full of frogspawn, frogspawn was
like sago, I preferred custard, mass would soon be over and we
could have our dinner. Little things can be very important
when you have to go to mass or when you're hungry. Do
you know what I realised at mass one Sunday? I often said lists
at mass, lists can pass the time, but I tried to say appropriate
lists, the commandments, for instance. Susan, I found out that
the commandments don't apply to us at all unless we're les-
bians. 'Thou shall not covet thy neighbour's wife . . .' See!
And they're all addressed to the same Thou, so! It changed
my life, Susan, I can tell you. Now, if I wrote a book, I'd like,
on our behalf, to admit a few things. I have slain my children,
sent my sons to war, peed in a cup in a guesthouse – mind you,
I scalded the cup in the morning in case people got germs –
made love with a dog, mind you, I put the dog down afterwards in case it thought that people were for making love to.
That shocks you, Susan? Well, they have pictures of people
and animals making love on temple and church walls all over
the world; of course, it's different in stone than in words, you
can blame stone easier. I did pray that my sons came home
from war even if they'd killed someone else's son and I kept
my mouth shut about the slain children, in case it encouraged
other women. No, I'd be OK. As long as I kept the stories ridiculous, no one would believe me. If I wrote that I jumped or

flew over buildings as a means of getting around, they'd say
that I had a wonderful capacity to make the fantastic real, but
if I started my book by saying that I had been blessed with two
things in my life, an active imagination and a wet cunt, if
you'd call that a blessing, now that would be different, they'd
say that everything in the book must have happened to me, I
couldn't possibly have dreamt them up. Jump buildings and
fly about all over the place, grand, but the other! So you're
right, Susan, I'd have to be careful. There are people in books
who take their tragedies out to have a look at them, or they
take their hearts out to throw them away because of the trouble they've caused. Me? I'd take the whole lot out just to have a
peep and if it turned into a gawk ... well. Nothing wrong
with a genuine gawk as long as you don't start looking for answers. Did you like history at school, Susan? Did you like Parnell? I loved Parnell and Kitty, I would have loved to have
done Michael Collins, I hated the Thirty Years War; anyway,
I don't believe any of it any more – if they lied about the rest,
I'm sure they lied about that too. I wouldn't write history, it's
just selected bits of news, doesn't teach you anything unless
you add it to other things, or at least the subject that they
passed off on us as history didn't teach us anything. Where do
they get the news? I hate the news. It's always about war or the
possibility of war, or the aftermath of war. It's always to
frighten us. If there wasn't any news, some of these men might
behave themselves better. They drown us with news from
places that have nothing to do with us, it gives them a way
out of doing something about that funny-looking thing on
their own doorsteps. They spend their time, these news gath-
erers, making sure that we don't enjoy ourselves. They depress
us at night, and tomorrow, what does it matter? In the evenings in newspaper offices the mothers go home, followed
soon after by the single women, who aren't that interested in

war, really. The single men and the fathers stay on, the fathers,
too, because when they were single men they always worked
all night, so not working all night is not an issue for discussion.
It's true, Susan, the bomb was always just about to be dropped,
women lay in muck up to their tonsils because of it; then it
wasn't going to happen, we were all about to go on an everlasting holiday, but no, next thing they're at it again. All those
men up at night couldn't let is rest. Get them to bed, Susan, on
their backs, I say; it's the only way to keep them out of doing
us harm. Make them stick to recipes and patterns, that's what I
say, Susan. I spent a night with a journalist once, had sex with
him. I don't think he was able to take his mind off his work. I
watched three seconds of him coming before I came myself.
His eyes were open, he hung on for dear life, paralysed with
pleasure, then he sailed away, hang-glided away, on the fright
of it. Afterwards I sensed that he loved it but didn't like the
intimacy of it. That's when I discovered how they get the
news. They stay up all night, even after sex, because they've
figured out that it's not night everywhere else. Later on, towards dawn, when a hurricane blew up in me again and
needed melting, he said no, that he was busy, he had to write
about how things affect the poor, that means the drop-outs,
the mentally ill, the homeless, the unemployed. I asked him
did he think that I didn't know who the poor are and did he
really think that they'd tell him. I wouldn't, partly because I'd
want to put my best side forward for him. Admitting the details of your poverty is not the most attractive thing on earth.
Still, I must say, they do a good job, those men who stay up at
night, so that people like me from nowhere will know nearly
immediately that Kennedy was shot. Yet I'm not sure. Who
wants to know who's killing who when you're supposed to
be dancing or asleep? No, I wouldn't write about history. In
history we were taught about the famine and I agree we need

to know but only if it teaches us that it didn't have to happen and never does; and we were taught that some of the Highlands were terribly badly cleared and we need to know that too, but what weren't we told? that's what I'd like to know, Susan. I used to read books to find out but I'm afraid there was nothing in them. Susan, do you think we're ordinary women? A man rang *The Late Late* one night and said that there were no ordinary women on the panel, he wanted an ordinary woman like his wife, but his wife's probably like us, Susan, and he doesn't know it. I think we're ordinary women, Susan. We weren't sexually abused as children, in fact I'd say our fathers pushed us away years too early just in case. It was nice standing there between their legs in the front of the hired car on our way to Granny's. Of course, you probably got a bus, we had to hire a car to see Granny. I wasn't starved either. Once, we had to eat porridge for our dinner, only once – I couldn't eat the bloody stuff even at breakfast time, it made me retch – mostly we had plenty of potatoes and cabbage. One day I suggested we have our dinner outside. Our mother agreed, which is not a usual thing for mothers to do, agree to the extraordinary. I had got the old coats spread out in the garden, I had left the pan down, full with the beautiful fried cabbage and potato. I was on my way in to get forks; the dog ate the whole of it, must have been in three seconds flat. My ears can still sting at the thought of what followed. If I was an actor and needed to cry, I'd have no problem, I'd just think of the day the dog ate the dinner. As well, my mother made me come home from school early, the minute it was finished I had to come home. What for? I always asked myself. What for? It wasn't as if there was anything at home. People with good memories make good mothers. I'd never make my children come home from school early for nothing. But I am an ordinary woman, well, as ordinary as anyone can be, considering I was nowhere the night

John F. was killed, and the lives we've lived since and the lies we've been told. A person is only ordinary when they're slipping out of the womb and haven't been told anything yet. What did this man think an ordinary woman was? A woman who has read only a few books? A woman who has a few books but has never read any of them? A woman who has read the books that give her only the right words? For instance, I don't use the word 'foetus', I think I'm committing a sin if I do, I'm inciting to murder. As I said, Susan, stay quiet about the slaying. How could anyone be an ordinary woman; our mothers when they were children were sent out of rooms when a baby boy's nappy was being changed, Mother of Divine Jesus, it's no wonder some of us pick at penises as if they were going to bite us. Ordinary? Ordinary? How could there be such a thing, how could any woman ever give a guarantee that she won't go berserk some night and smash up the town? Which is why, Susan, I'm now going to change our drinks. I'm going to order champagne for us and tell you what I think we are that was never said in the books I read. First, the state of us, it varies so much there is no possibility of describing it, the picture makes no sense. So let's say, Susan, we are of such indeterminate sizes, measurements, proportions, that we are best left with names as a means of pointing us out. We are sometimes fat, thin, heavy-breasted, flat-chested, high-hipped; we are sometimes droopy with lust and drowsy with love; we are fast, we are tight, we are so loose the wind could blow a hole in our fannies. But the shape of us is not important. We love sex, we go wild for it at times, but you'd never guess by what they've said, now would you? We were stalking this country in the nineteen fifties, early sixties, pleasuring ourselves and them. Well, I know you and I weren't, Susan, only because it was before our time, but those lovely women, let's say, over in that corner, those women with the silver veins on their cheekbones, they were, but that's not what the books said. The books made us saints, cheap, plastic saints with lack of love, or they called us scarlet, but they didn't see it as a real colour. No Irish book ever told me about love unless it was referring to carvings on church walls, back to the stone, Susan, it's safer. Do they think we wouldn't claw the earth for someone to turn to us at night and say, 'Do you like it this way?' sliding hands down around us, or that we wouldn't on a lonesome, not lonely, night turn to a body next to us and say, 'My place', there are a lot of Saturday nights to be got through? Or that we don't do it to ourselves? Crawl out of our single beds some mornings not fit to move? Do they think we only want what they've forced us to say is love, that we don't want a hand running up and down our clitoris as if trying to find it, a good warm breast that we can touch by putting our hands up a wide sleeve, that we don't want a finger with a grabbable wrist at the bottom of it, piff! one finger, three fingers, up our wombs, or maybe a man above, below, across us on a rainy night, determined to make us weak with wanting him? I ask you, Susan, how come the men who write don't know us? The men do. Look at him, Susan, no, not him, I don't like men with turned-up cuffs, not until I've spoken to them at least, the man beside him. I once thought that I'd write to Mr Miller. Mr Miller, to get straight to the point, you don't know your arse from your elbow, so to speak. It's not a door you're in bed with, it's not a tight blank hole, it's not a gap – a gap is only a between thing – it's not meat. Meat? You're fooling yourself beyond the beyond. Not on purpose, of course, it's because you understand so little, you think you could eat it; it's the other way about, Mr Miller. Although you'd never say it, I'm sure that's what you fear and you have reason. A cunt, not spoken to properly, could turn on you and where would you be then? You caught halfway up and no way of getting out.

Careful, Mr Miller, I say, careful. What is wrong with you that you must do unto, ram, convince yourself? Why are you so afraid of sex? Why must you believe you have pulled a fast one? Why must you make perversion out of passion and importance? That wild imploring look, could you perhaps have read it wrong? I only ask. Mr Miller, there are few of us who would not have cheered you on if you had enjoyed yourself. And remembered names. Were you simply looking for applause or trying to get a reputation around town and were you perhaps an erotic intimate under the candles? Mr Miller, why is it that you cannot bear us to enjoy it as much, or even worse, more than you? It is hard for you to know that sex is not forbidden to us. We have got permission and it's not from you, it's from ourselves, all sorts, all shapes of us. The call boy in you can pretend he's making the calls but your money's running out. Now! Making love, Mr Miller, that's for grown-ups, a creating of a shadow in someone's eyes, a passing of the hand lightly over the down on someone's face, so near to skin and yet not touching it. You know, we do everything, we kiss across bottoms, we drive you mad with the loss of your and our senses, we like it, Henry, although you wish we didn't. Susan, I'd tell him about the things we've done; look at the things you've done, Susan, and no one would think it to look at you, no offence, Susan, you're beautiful, it's not that, it's the way you stand and the way you don't look at people, that's what would make people doubt. I'd tell him, Susan, that fucking isn't mere background noise to us. (Of course, I shouldn't single only Mr Miller out.) I'd tell him that I knew only one man ever who could make love properly and it wasn't him. This man, who I knew, could make love by looking at me. On our first night, summer came in the dead of winter, the light coming through the window changed from watery black to red-yellow. In the restaurant afterwards we sat with our

elbows on the table, eventually, leaning over, we matched our
wrists, spread our hands together then joined our fingers. We
would never be the same again, we were close enough to hurt
each other by thinking. I should have been careful about that
but how can you think when you're filling up with heartbeats?
We made love all the time because that was the only word we
had which seemed adequate to explain the torrential thing that
happened to us; we couldn't get enough of each other, we
drank our sweat, we to-ed and fro-ed, emptying one into the
other, like children will when they play with jugs of water.
We melted into a single body and sometimes couldn't figure
out where one of us started and the other ended. His eyes
filmed over when I came into a room. I could always see that,
in the first second, before my own filmed so badly I could see
almost nothing. I could feel my clothes on me all the time. As
the months went on we got scared, I often put my hands
around his wrists, my thumb and middle finger would overlap
because I have large hands. I did this deliberately because I
thought it might bring me back to earth the way simple
touches sometimes can. The bed we lay on – the floorboards
many times because we couldn't always wait – took notes. I
wonder did it ever warn me? I remember once in particular,
this was before disappointment, we made love in his work-
room, we could do it without a sound, if we had to, so the
people beyond the four-inch partition would think we were
reading or staring into each other's eyes at the most. We kissed
quietly, touching our teeth, a voice that surely wasn't mine
spoke to me, my blood made noise, he came high up into me
as easily as you write 'Dear' at the beginning of a letter, before
you know what will happen. His phone rang, persistently, so
he came out of me and walked across the room. His penis was
covered with my blood, giving us all the comfort we needed.
We had already bled into each other, so this did not come as a

surprise. As he spoke on the phone I came over him again and he turned inside me, making me a long warm shiver. He is gone now but that's another story. When I think of making love I think of his thumb held on my spine from inside, held there as a reminder, him smiling as if he didn't know what he was doing. I know where he was the night Kennedy was shot. That's the sort of thing I'd tell Mr Miller and he could show the letter to his buddies. Christ, there's my bloody landlord and I'm three weeks behind. Hello, Patrick, how are you? Come on, Susan, let's get out of here before he starts. Let's go to my place and read some books. Books you've never heard of, books we can grow up to. You don't have to go home yet, you can stay up late for once. Of course I will, for you, Susan, anything. I suppose you're right, he wouldn't show the letter to his buddies. Still, you'd never know.

THE LONG DROP

Thomas McGurk knew that people got more confident with age, that they were able to tackle the small matters in life as if they were what they were. Or he thought he knew. But herein lay a problem, he wasn't sure any more if what he knew or thought he knew was right. Indeed, he knew nothing for certain these days. Take his last visit to the dentist. He had punched in his time in the waiting room building himself up, speaking positively to himself. But then a stray thought had donated itself. If Mr Rattigan said to him again, 'Oh dear, there is no problem with your teeth, but your gums, your gums! Your teeth will last you your lifetime, but your gums! Mind you, your lifetime, hmmm, still smoking I see, hmmm', he would say, Look here, you're my dentist, that's all, and I'm paying you to look after my teeth, to service my mouth, so to speak, so stop your lecturing and get on with the job. But he only wanted to say that. When it came to the bit, he knew he wouldn't, he hadn't got the nerve. And he used not mind what the dentist said, but now he had actually become afraid of that lecture, unable to answer it. He should say, 'See here you, Mr Rattigan, I do not think it's any of your business what I do with my mouth or any other part of me. Stick on your gloves and your protective mask and floss away to your heart's content. And by the way, could you cease making provocative statements while my mouth is being held open by the mini walking stick that you've just thrown over my teeth.'

Dead, that's the only way he'd ever say it. For the last six months he couldn't say boo to a goose. This might be a problem for any person but for Thomas it was a disaster because his job was in PR. That's right, he thought, I'm supposed to be a PR man. A man who knows everything, a constantly busy, important man.

The queue dwindled slowly. He was glad of this and yet he wanted to be out of there. Decisive! He was also having night-mares. In the last one he had been a participant in a simple quiz show on television. He had answered only one out of thirty-five questions. Sweat had poured down the screen. The whole country had been watching him, including his first girlfriend and other, unrecognisable girlfriends whom he never knew he had. Waking up had not brought him consolation, had instead worried him further. A PR man. A man who knows every-thing, a man who can be handed any fact, who can then take that fact away on a private walk and do with it whatever he wants, a man who is too busy to notice the unimportant goings-on of the ordinary unimportant people who walk up and down his road. So what had this exceptionally important man achieved so far that day?

Breakfast had been eaten quickly – the less said the better being his motto at that hour in the morning. On one side of him was his good-looking son, who picked his way through breakfast, and everything else, as if he owned the world and had bought the table. Yes, the less said the better. On the other side of him, his ageing father, who was visiting for a week. Thomas McGurk was being storm-destroyed, youth and seni-lity were filling his arteries this morning, leaving no time for his own age. He had then gone to foreign exchange at the bank. The customer in front of him was talking twenty to the dozen, telling all her business. Maybe she was a widow and had no one to talk to at home. The bank teller appeared to be listening. The customer told him loudly, cheerfully, at the top of her voice range, like a chorister, that she wanted separate pesetas for the two children, for their own pocket money, you know what I mean, plenty of notes if possible, preferably not the ten thousand ones – this by way of indicating that she roughly knew the denominations in question. Or that she had children, or that she was going, could afford to go, on a holiday. What was he doing listening to this claptrap? What was he doing coming into the bank in the first place, when he had more important things to be doing?

'That was a terrible accident,' she said, 'of eleven of them only seven were found, they were killed as well as drowned.'

He was in the bank getting sterling for his trip to London. He could use his card and get it out of a machine at the other end, but banks could be comforting; going to foreign exchange marked the importance of country leaving, set differences between one journey and another. It would be a terrible thing if they ever brought in the ecu. Or he could easily have asked his wife to get him the money. For some reason, she had the height of respect for him, the last person to suffer from that, he hiccuped to himself. He went to the counter, did his business, chatted amicably enough to the clerk, got his changed money. Such a transaction! This paper is worth that. Now can you give me someone else's paper worth the same. And different people accrued different amounts of paper for living the same lives. There was a lot to Marx.

He should be looking at the ads on the wall. He was a PR man, he should be interested. But he could only look at the woman sitting at the back desk in the office, not that he thought her good-looking, but because she seemed so

organised, so engrossed, she must be content. There was a
flawless rhythm about the way she lifted the telephone, tapped
her computer, put down the phone, reached for papers, for
statements, and it was herself who had worked out that
rhythm. Yes, he should be interested in the ads, maybe he
could make an ad out of her. He didn't make ads as such, but
keeping the new successful ones just under his skin at his temple was part of his job in PR. The successful ad would tell you
how to pitch your next product. A good PR man could sell
anyone anything, could make anyone believe. He used to be
able to do so himself. And now? Now he had to hesitate before
having a conversation with his wife. This would have to stop.
After seeing the dentist, he would go to the office, find out
about the new contract he'd be working on in London. He
would cheer up, cheer himself up, take his wife out to dinner,
pack his clothes for the next day, sleep well, have no dreams.

That must have been three months ago, no, longer than
that, because it was while he was in London that it had really
started, or maybe that's when he had noticed just how smack
bang up against the wall he was. The day had been too hot for
May, from his window the street looked like a cramped smo-
ky pub. There must have been a shortage of air, because people
had paused by railings, when they found them, and gasped, as
if they were in hospital corridors. He left his hotel to go to see
de Kooning at the Tate, which almost rhymed with 'Beckett at
the Gate', a poem he'd just read. He'd started to do this recently, at first to impress clients, or his PR colleagues. 'De
Kooning at the Tate' would sound good. But there was a danger that some of it could seep in, that he would find himself
standing in front of a picture longer than was necessary, that
he would begin dropping into bookshops casually, that he
would begin to believe poems.

He'd read about the de Kooning exhibition in the

Independent, the English one, on Sunday. At home in bed. He came to the arts pages, usually at twelve thirty or so, that's Monday really, but it still feels like a Sunday night. A few minutes after the arts pages comes the 'How We Met' spot. He hated it, just as much as he used to hate 'Family Ties' in the *Sunday Tribune*, where one family member waxed on about another, shone things up, glossed over their real selves. He knew the tricks. He knew a man who had done it once; he'd tried to be analytical, but they had managed to change the tone by letting a word or two slip, or so the man said, but Thomas didn't believe him. He happened to know that the man hadn't spoken to his brother for years, that there was a rotting thing between them, a thing that would have been smellable from the next townland if they'd lived in wide open spaces where smells could be separated. Thomas didn't know much about de Kooning, nothing in fact, he didn't mind admitting to himself, but he liked the name and got fixated for the few moments that it took him to read the article. He checked the dates. He would go see it on his next visit to London, it would fit in. He considered these fixations to be every bit as reasonable as love.

So there he was now on the tube, reading the bad thriller he'd bought at the airport. Even his wife had done more dangerous things in her life than the woman who had got herself murdered in the book. He lifted his eyes too often to check the next station, the names not staying with him long enough, making him look like a stranger. He was a stranger.

Last month he'd gone to the hospital with his father, supposedly to find out for the rest of the family what these tests would say, what exactly the matter was, but he had skulked in the waiting area for as long as possible, not wanting to be told about body parts, nor hear his father talk about this and that and sigh that ten years ago there hadn't been too much wrong with him. Before setting off for the appointment, he'd had a moment of caring and had offered to bring breakfast to bed for the old man, but, of course, his father had insisted on getting up to have it with him, stealing his privacy, telling him to lift that good coat, making him a child in front of his own child, who didn't notice either of them. There was a new nightmare that came often, the coat hangers rattling on the back of their bedroom door, signalling his father walking in on top of them.

In the hospital his father had looked at the man across the room, 'Put you in mind of Mary's Liam.'

'I don't know,' Thomas had snapped, and then tried to take the sting away by attempting to laugh, 'And couldn't care less'. How brave of him to be bullying an old man. He was nearly overcome by the grief of not caring. He knew that the old man's neighbour took two hot-water bottles to bed, but kept the windows and doors open for fresh air. Very important that. How he knew was obvious, he had been told. Many times. Silly womanish things that the old man would have told his wife if she had still been alive; most likely it was she who had said them in the first place and he was repeating them now to his personal vacuum. He'd been told lots of other things too, of no importance any of them, clogging up thinking space and the telling of them clogging up time. He knew so much useless information, he needed a personal drainage system from his brain. When your head got full of useless information did you keel over? Did old really mean a head more full of memory than expectation?

His father had made a county council cottage into a thing almost resembling a bungalow, so surely Thomas could be a PR man. He would PR his way out of every corner. Remember that brave boy who had jumped into the dying bus driver's seat and slammed on the brakes in time to stop a catastrophe?

It was on the TV. Apparently he couldn't be brave again and it was expected of him. Word is, he couldn't repeat himself. Well, neither could Thomas. Thomas had lost his PR skills. In the ward, where they were now settling his father into a bed, more tests to be done, the old man prattled away the nervous waiting and Thomas knew not of what he spoke. He was a stranger indeed.

He got off at the right station and went to the art gallery, where he saw a woman who walked around beautifully, the trousers clinging to her, like silk does to a woman. Watching her was almost unbearable. In truth, he was glad to get out of the de Kooning exhibition. The painter neither upset nor pleased him. He went to a café, where he watched his accent – you could never tell the temperature of Anglo-Irish relations. It was best to avoid confrontation. He got sad for himself. Could loneliness get worse than this? He was growing for his grave, waiting around to have his name fitted on a headstone. Of course he was a PR man. But what did that mean? When he was young, a woman had disappeared from his parish, a woman not quite right, leaving behind a brother who was even less right. A telegram arrived, 'Miss Mary Bell alive and well in Belgium'. Her brother repeated it like a mantra down through the years. A man his own age, who became a European, saw the same Mary Bell, destitute in Brussels, at the age of sixty. He decided to tell no one, except Thomas. It would be better for neighbours to think of her as alive and well. Thomas wished that he hadn't been told.

After the café, Thomas went to his meeting. The client wanted to advertise in Ireland, the economy was doing well there, the papers said so. He wanted a space theme; what did Thomas think? What did Thomas think about space? Here's what he thought. He couldn't cope with his own sitting room. The client had been in Ireland ten years ago. He asked questions appropriate to that experience and for a few moments Thomas was fine. The tricks of happiness include explaining to strangers the politics of one's country to one's own satisfaction, leaving out the aggravating truths. In Berlin and Jerusalem this is allowed – places where it is clear that there is no such thing as the Truth, that all truth depends on perspective. In the client's office, for five minutes, Thomas talked like a citizen of one of those cities, or Belfast. In hotels at night, in strange countries, you can draw maps to show the bar staff where you were born in relation to Dublin and the border. They won't know that you've got the shape of the country all wrong.

The client looked like his brother-in-law, the one who had ME – all those years in bed had given him a youthful look. Had his client had ME, or was he in fact just young? What did this man know about Ireland? Did he know that they were now growing pot plants in the country, for God's sake? Thomas had noticed them on his last journey to the midlands, where he'd stayed in a damp hotel. Soon he wouldn't have to worry about his teeth being gone, they would just be gone. When he was young he was always out making things happen. There had been a vastness of time in front of him, he could have been anything, he could have become gay, could have become a light person.

'We will go out and make things happen,' the client said.

'Indeed we will,' said Thomas, buttoning up his coat, snapping closed his briefcase, backing out the door, afraid to walk face first. Leaving the building, he thought, I don't want to actually be a bird, I just want to fly.

On the street a church bell rang continuously as if six funerals were arriving. A singing busker looted her life for the emotions of her song. If she were on a real stage, could she have ambition? Thomas used to have that unfailingly dependent desire to master the next goal, to get the next most important job, to meet key people. And he had met them. But the trouble is that when you know hordes of people, you know more people who get sick, and more people who die. He had been good at his job, very good, so good he was hated. Not for him the useless pity of the encyclopaedia seller who tells the destitute pensioner that, on second thoughts, she cannot afford his books. If there was a man in the room who might be useful sometime, he got buried in him in two seconds flat. And made sure that no one else got near him. Now getting a taxi was an achievement. But if he got one, maybe he could stay in it. Not yet.

Thomas saw the church and sidled in. He had left all that palaver behind him ages ago. The smell was still the same. The silence was still the same. That's what he needed. Silence. Total silence. He had talked too much in his lifetime, laid silence to waste in his job. All those sentences. The air was still the same. He sat in the back row and fell asleep. If he expired here, they would whisper to each other at home, Did you hear that he died in the chapel. That's a good one, isn't it?

A LITTLE REMOTE

She left her job and her organised life with an ease that surprised herself more than anyone else. It was martyrdom, but it didn't feel like it. Lucy Skipplestow was off to mind her widowed, retired businessman father. The sea would be there. The west coast of Ireland greyness might lodge in her brain – in the winter damp it might burrow into her bones – but when the sun shone she could think herself anywhere. Sometimes the sky and the sea were one. The ocean was the clouds and the grey clouds were really seaweed. A skyful of white foam stretching for all the visible miles can make anyone's day seem more important than it is. Lucy should not have gone back so easily – she should have been more concerned about her job, her flat, her life – but something other than guilt made her.

Friends would take over her rooms. Her job would always be there for her, her reference was eulogistic. Her life could wait. What much was it anyway? A lover here and there, often more trouble than they were worth. She could have fun and friends anywhere, because what was the difference between one shared laugh and another, one chat and another? So she told herself. She didn't dwell on her belief that it probably wouldn't be for long. She had set his death scene long before the thought had entered his head or his body. Lucy, blessed with unusual luck, had said what she had to say to her mother before she died. She needed to say something to Mr Skipplestow, or at least to try.

She did try, but he wasn't used to listening to other people, certainly not women. His life had always been a business, time was a profit or a loss. He would have built a bunker, for investment in it, but people might have laughed at him. Anyway, he would surely be able to die a natural death, and Lucy should look after herself. So she cooked for him and drove him, washed and prepared his food, living in separate blocks which came together to make a day, a week, a month, in the receding life of Mr Skipplestow. (And Lucy.)

She returned happily to an old hobby and discovered that she was better at it than she had remembered. She painted large pictures in her room on canvases that were sometimes a foot taller than herself. She stretched to put in stars and birds, or peered at yellow whins and wondered if they were maybe too golden. She smiled a lot to herself each time she finished a picture.

In the beginning she bought frames only when she was shopping alone. Then she chose them with her father. Later, Mr Skipplestow bought them for her, not for any serious reason, but because there was not much point in painting pictures if you didn't frame them. Once, he looked at some of the canvases in her room. He was surprised that there were so many of them. Lucy liked the smell of paint and it passed some time. She would not get notions about herself.

When her father's brother died, she prepared to go to the funeral with a little excitement. A night in her old flat in Dublin, the boat journey to Holyhead, a train speeding to London. She arranged to meet Bernard on her way back. She would be gone for almost a week and the funeral didn't really bother her because she had not been close to her uncle.

Her flat startled her in some way. She stood in the doorway and thought about the strange ways she'd grown up inside these rooms. She had experienced ecstasy, small pieces of love, and some loneliness here. Past experiences became animate objects and seemed to look down on her from the corners of the ceilings. Her friends were keeping it well. They all went for a drink. There were people everywhere; Lucy got drunk on them. There were friends of hers from minor pasts that she'd forgotten about – it's funny how many pasts a person can have and it still makes only one. They were all here to see her, up from the country, which made her worry that perhaps she was doing an odd thing. Was it really so? She worried that perhaps it was.

There were so many people, so many people, to pick from. She could talk to any of them, any one of them, and there would be more after that. How wonderful! Was there a time in her life when she had kissed strange men? Been kissed, and more? When she herself had taken initiatives, despite the risks of being turned down? Had she once bought satin sheets? Surely not! She felt awkward among these people who were at ease carnally with each other – you could tell, they moved their bodies past and around each other without saying excuse me. Back in the spare room she fell asleep quickly, protecting herself from too much wondering.

It was a relief to get on the boat, to be pulled away from the shore. What was the difference between her now and one year ago? Could it be that strange? Could she have become strange? She would have time to think. She supposed there was not much point in thinking about the painting.

The boat smelled of recent vomiting, but the sea was kind on this journey. Lucy bought a ticket for the Pullman lounge and sat with the individuals on the boat, the people who had big jobs, big cars, and big everythings, away from the emigrants and their conversations. She'd had those on every other journey over. Emigrants always talked, blabbered in fact, terrified that they were making a mistake. Women who didn't talk and looked ahead of themselves were not emigrants. There were always a few of them on the boat, holding themselves together. Lucy read some, slept some, tasting her hangover. She had tea, read some more. She didn't now want to think.

Two men talked loudly; bulging with confidence, she thought bitterly. Should she be minding a man like them beside the sea? Had they or he ever done anything for her? How did they see her, they or he? He saw her, in fact, for her daughterly use. He didn't know much about her, but that didn't bother him. They, these two, didn't notice her at all. They were gone past noticing every woman. Lately they only looked at the ones that they felt they could get without much bother, between matters of a serious nature, on the rare occasions that they were moved to it now.

Lucy was glad to get on the train. Her journey was becoming layered relief. She watched England pass her window, trying not to think about the desolation of Crewe or Chester. But maybe the train stations were giving the wrong impression. Maybe Crewe was full of people in love. Perhaps away from the station there were narrow streets and cosy front rooms. She swallowed the foul-tasting artificial tea – you couldn't cheat by taking tea bags because the cups were pre-filled. She should have thought of a flask. But was she that old? She looked well, all of her, her face in particular. Perhaps her body gestures were a little hurried, she needed to hold back sometimes from something, maybe from disgracing herself.

At Rugby a family boarded. The small girl sat in the now vacant seat beside her. People had come and gone at stations and Lucy had avoided all conversation, but a child was harmless.

'Can I see your book?' she asked. As she flicked through it she discovered that it was a horrifying tale of missionaries and of God's wrath on a black pagan boy. The family were heavy Christian. The child did not trust her, could sense Lucy's doubt about the story. She slunk to the other seat to her father's knee. An older child hissed at her not to disturb him because he was praying. She came back to Lucy's seat.

Could Lucy say anything that might endear her to the girl? She could feel her anger rising at those people, at those parents, who could tell the child whatever they liked, especially in the name of God, because they were parents, and she, Lucy, was no one. Her no-oneness silenced her. Why should she care anyway? Who were these people to her? And children?

Later the mother read the story aloud – the black pagan was helped by Christians because he was gradually losing his sight; he did go blind, despite the help, but 'Wasn't he better, dear, to be blind and to know Jesus than to be a pagan?' Whatever you say, you lovely logical adult you. The child looked terrified but she might give up her job when she was older to take care of them; then again she might murder them.

Euston drew towards them rhythmically, as if the train and London were two people rushing towards each other. Passengers jumped out of carriages as if scalded and dashed out of exit gates, never once bumping into one another. Lucy was not a bewildered stranger to this station scene. She had been to London often and in fact she loved it. She was also glad to be off the train. Surely that would be the last of the reliefs. Three chirpy people held a banner above their heads. Lucy passed them, then turned curiously to see what she could already hear, an enthusiastic welcome, the sort that always jolts the lone traveller. It was for the Christians. She was disappointed. She met her own relations, shook hands and left for the funeral parlour.

'How is your father?'

Why couldn't they call him by his name?

'Fine.'

'You must find it a little remote?'

'No. Not really. I paint.'

What a thing to say!

The attendant was Irish – not from Dublin. He walked towards the body, his hands down in his pockets, with the awkwardness of a country man in his Sunday suit on a Tuesday. His face was not heart-failure blue, but rather a raw red that had worked its way deeper than skin in a place miles, oh centuries, from here. His reverence and discretion grated on Lucy, yet she knew she should allow him these, as well as his moment of victory, one London Irish standing over one dead London Irish.

Her uncle lay mocking her by his resemblance to her own father. She could hear his voice clearly, now that she saw him before her, a soft London overtone, urging her mother not to be such a square, at some past family gathering. He was the wild one. He had a dimple and it had suited him.

They left the freezing room and made their way to the distant cousins' flat where Lucy would stay. Relations were gathering and were being accommodated here and there with clinical precision. Now that the viewing of the body was over, she could look at the colour of London. It was always good for her.

Her cousin was having some people to dinner. It had been too late to cancel, so the mourners were mixed with the guests. A lazy stiltedness hampered the free flow of conversation, but Lucy didn't mind – she was enjoying herself because she could afford to judge lives now that she was away from her own. The man was at the bottom corner of the table, she thought

now, but she couldn't be sure because, true, she had not noticed him immediately. Later she drifted into conversation
with him. She'd had better conversations in her life; she'd had
worse. Some relation whom Lucy had never met interrupted.

'Your father couldn't come. Of course. It's nice for him to
have you.' A sad, piqued little voice making some point
known only to itself.

The man – Desmond, Desmond Palmer – moved away.

'How do you like the change to the country?' the relation
continued. This person knew everything. Who was he?

'I'm your father's cousin once removed. You remember
Francis and Kevin, on holidays? My sons. You were small, of
course. Solicitors and doctors now.'

'Oh yes, I do, now that I think about it.'

No word of his other son Brendan. What had he done
wrong?

The man Desmond – Desmond Palmer – came back.

'Will it be possible for you to socialise during your stay?' he
said.

'I thought that's what I was doing.'

They laughed. The once removed cousin left.

'No, I mean, really socialise.'

'Perhaps the night after tomorrow night. I wasn't close to
my uncle.' She had almost forgotten why she was here.

'The night after? Why not come to my house for dinner tomorrow night? The night after seems too late if you only have
a few days.'

'Why not.'

*Dear Desmond. I wish I could write to you about how I'm feeling, how
I'm remembering, but I cannot do that, now that I know you do not feel
the same way. You said that women get more hurt out of these things, or
was it me who said that? If I was writing to you, I could tell you many*

*things. I could remind you of what you said to me when I said that I
wasn't in the habit of doing this. Then again, I probably wouldn't –
no, I would leave that aside, why shouldn't I? Because no shyness, no
fear stopped me, I have no need to make excuses. We didn't know that
we didn't know each other. You might think that I have a remarkable
memory; I would reply that memory is the vicious tragedy of not being
able to forget.*

Lucy enjoyed dinner, there was a smell of wine from the sauce.
There was music; he had brandy. He had done this before. But
no. Well perhaps, well perhaps a few times. They laughed. He
told her about bringing his mother back to Ireland. She had
not been there since she was twenty. Lucy could see it. He
had driven her to the townland. She directed him. She had said
that maybe they should stop here and see if this neighbour was
still alive. They had asked tactfully. The seventy-five-year-old
woman called to the field: 'John, there is someone to see you.'
No jealousy left now where there was at least life. John moved
away from the scythe, then thought better of it and took it
with him so as not to appear too enthusiastic. He and Desmond's mother were eighty-one. He left his hand where it
was, cupping grass on the ditch. He squinted at her and
drawled in the voice of a twenty-year-old: 'Is that you, Babs?'
Then he kissed her, his wrinkled lips touched her cheeks that
were well beyond wrinkling any more: 'I've waited sixty years
to do that.' They chuckled. She said later, 'And he kissed me
with his wife standing at the door. Ach well, I suppose.' Outside the cowshed that had been their school. They left after tea
and snaps reverently taken.

   'I can get you the photo,' Desmond said.
   'Do please.'
   'This is the house where she was born. Do you know
Mayo?' There was a lake in front of the house. His mother

had slapped her bag twice on her thigh and said, 'Happy memories, happy memories.'

Lucy told him that she painted and that her father read the
deaths in the paper every morning. Desmond asked questions
about her painting. What colours did she like best? Did she
paint mostly people or landscape? Did her women look out?
Had she read John Berger? She answered expansively all his
questions, all of them – how wonderful to be asked – and yes,
she had read John Berger.

They laughed more. They slipped into bed. She touched
him, but he could only think of being up and inside her. He
knew nothing about lovemaking as such, about nearness.
Strange, was that why he had shown her the other photographs of his last holiday in Athens? Him surrounded by
women. Who was he trying to tell what? I may not be able
to make love but I always have a woman. Photographs of holidays at their age! There wasn't much caressing, and what there
was of it seemed to be without physical connection, perfunc-
tory rubbing until he could get inside. His own body was cold
as steel with only one feeling part to it. The man who had
taken his mother back! She tried running her fingers over his
shoulders, butterfly movements on his chest. Too light. OK
then, stronger, stronger touching from his toes to his ears,
kiss-sucking his nipples. She shivered. It was like communion
with a corpse. All right then, if that's what you want, do please
enter. I will take you in and wrap myself around you so you
can be safe. And when he did come in he was grateful. He
wanted to put out the light.

'Why?' she asked.

'Because if I make love with you without the light on, the
dark will never be as bad again.'

'What is your house in the west like?' Desmond asked her in
the morning, waking her gently.

'Big windows. Quiet.'

'Your town?'

She could see the Sunday session in the local pub. She didn't want to. Not this morning. Begrudging people. How could she explain, without letting them down, that they were afraid in the summer, when their cruel wintry life came face to face with holiday-makers? It would be a pity to sell them short in this plush room. She said nothing about them and talked instead of blue skies, when they were blue, green fields, the sun, the colour of clothes. Her voice seemed nervous as it came out into the quiet . . .

'I want to be inside you again.'

Dear me, Lucy thought. She felt herself getting into trouble. It seemed as if cloudy bits inside her head were melting, her blood was wet, slipping into places that had been dry for a while; like a teenager, she winced. But where caution warned her, she didn't listen.

She did wish him to say more, now that it was daylight, but he had brought her down to his size and didn't need to. (That was caution speaking to her.) Was he going to ask her to stay longer? She might have been expected to feel uncomfortable about some things – for instance, naked bodies, his and hers, the bathroom off the bedroom, french letters, the phone ringing – but the only thing that worried her was, did he want her to stay? Was she lively enough? She made love with him again, back to the wombing, because she felt so pleased when he asked her that it would have been a nonsense not to. But she felt his silence taking something from her. He could have looked at her all day, all the time, as he moved, hoping to chase away the reluctance in her, but she would not look back. She would not. She turned her head. He was undecided as to whether or not he should feel slighted or encouraged. He opted for the latter and felt worse for it. She withdrew, like a snail, taking her juices with her. Emptiness came into her.

He stopped the car three minutes before they got to her cousins' place to show that he was emotional.

'How does that prove anything?' she wondered aloud, perplexed.

'I didn't want to wait until we got there to say goodbye.'

There was a funeral to be gone to.

Desmond Palmer promised to ring Lucy Skipplestow before she left to go home to Ireland. He did not phone. Who knows why not? Lack of interest? Unlikely – some of his words suggested a lot of interest. Fear? Perhaps he thought that emotion was something to be allowed in the over-eighties, if they could still think by then and if they lived that long. Lucy Skipplestow was upset, in fact she was devastated, which she shouldn't have been because she should have known better, but since when has 'shouldn't' been 'isn't' or 'wasn't'?

Dear Desmond. Perhaps you did ring and I was out.

Lucy got on the train in a silent Euston. She hated him. There were curses and rages in her head. She fell asleep exhausted and woke holding his hand. She jumped from the seat to have tea and to shake him off but it was too late now to do that. She thought about nothing else through England, his face came with her the whole way. On the boat she sat on the same lounge seat, away from returning emigrants and still, silent women, yet she could not remember getting off the train.

Lucy tried to make herself concentrate on the short-comings...

He was lovely, she thought, bloody lovely.

That woman there, who is painting herself now, an hour from shore, she has had three children, all of them sons. She is painting herself to meet her in-laws. She is happy. Lucy would have to think about having a child, some day.

The steward turned away two children who wanted only to watch television. This was a paying room. He included Lucy in his scathing look to them – he thought she also wanted them gone, but she hadn't even seen them.

Somehow Ireland came into view. A call from ship to shore. Lucy does not wish to be landed.

Her flat seemed more welcoming this time. Lucy was subdued, defeated by chance. She wished she had some cold lever, some device to move her out of this wretchedness. A few days would surely help. She met Bernard – who was he? She focused and refocused her eyes, but could not remember him. He thought her distant and off-putting.

She did not wish to go west. A city at least offered some diversion. But she went, because she would not have to explain her foolishness there.

For a month she watched the postman. She felt a numbness and at the same time a silliness that was very alive. One morning she nearly prayed.

Dear Desmond. I wish I could phone you but I am afraid. I keep waiting for you to write. I cannot believe that you are not thinking of me at exactly the moments that I am thinking of you, which is, I'm afraid, often. How could you not be?

Seasons ran easily and predictably into each other. Lucy tagged her own life on to her father's. He wasn't, after all, so bad. Really, it wasn't that he didn't want to understand, perhaps he just couldn't. She painted large wild pictures with the women looking out. She often said the man's name when she was stroking on the last blue or yellow.

Desmond.

Dear Desmond. I sometimes think of you naked and how pleased you were. But it gets harder to remember. What is your face like? What colour are your eyes? Strange that you should have tried to impress on me so much that your life was all right, strange that you should have told me that you went to work whistling, an archaeologist, happy with the tenth century and ruins. Strange, because I believe that you are even unhappier than I. Do you have a beard, glasses, hair? I cannot remember.

The evening that she did ring, a year ago now, he sounded half-pleased, flattered, but closed, definitely closed. Lucy knew. Her own voice rang in her ears for hours afterwards, words like 'Lucy fool', then she calmed herself, better to know. He wasn't very brave. He would never have fitted in around here anyway.

Summer was good. The dry clouds lit up at night in pink and orange stripes. The traditional musicians played with less cocksureedness, shocked by the sun and the way it gave the women some extra secret. They changed to slow tunes because reels were made for winter. Lucy put some of the musicians under a pink cloud in a painting. She stood at the big quiet window wondering about colour, her legs a little apart. Normally she didn't notice how she stood but this morning she felt him between her thighs, the whole body of him, so she knew her feet must be apart. She felt him distinctly and heard his need to be inside. Her lips thinned, moved to the ends of her mouth, her eyes crinkled at the corners. It could have been called a smile. And then the pain came back, the memory of his eyes – that was the worst because it was so personal. Looking is very personal, Lucy thought.

Dear Desmond. Whatever you gave me, you didn't. I gave it to myself. You're only a tired spawn floating heavily in me.

Dear Desmond. That's from an old Italian poem. I didn't mean a word of it.

Her father died in January. He just couldn't pitch himself at another year. She held his hand and the next minute he was gone. Her heart split open and every woman and every man she'd ever loved passed through the crack, hitting off the edges as they went.

By the end of February Lucy had packed all her belongings ready to go back to Dublin. She wondered what the paintings would look like in a confined space, crushed into a city. She had gone to Dublin three times since the death. Bernard had helped her get the flat ready. She wanted to share the rooms with someone because she hoped to get a part-time job until such time as her clock could understand commerce again. Bernard seemed ideal, Lucy told him. He tried to show only the appropriate amount of delight. But first she would have a weekend in London.

Desmond had heard about her father's death, through the distant cousin, and had written her a letter. He was good at things like that, archaeology and old love. She would go now, because since her father's death she felt her full height, five feet eight inches. She decided not to tell Bernard and to leave wondering why not until later. She would be able for whatever did or didn't happen in London. For long enough now Lucy had watched the sun slipping out of the sky into the ocean and she had learned not to cling to it the way a child holds on to the hem of a skirt. In the west she had also learned about colour, old men and exiles.

Dear Desmond. Thank you for your letter. Certainly I'd be delighted to call on you next time I'm in London. As it so happens . . .

Exiles, men on the run, make love to their countrywomen high up in the womb, which is hard to get over, but Lucy had seen how the sun always comes up again from the other side of the sky and how it spends a whole day shining on skirts.

THE TOUR

They hung around Paris, wondering if there was a God, and indeed if they had just seen him. They had been here one day, this batch, representing the imagination of their country, which, of course, they believed had an incomplete existence, otherwise they would have gratefully put out the lights on their own. They were on a European tour, or at least a few of its countries, and with some luck they might remember it fondly. The workers who were putting the festival together were getting to know each other really well. The artists prevaricated between longing to be at home in their own beds and taking provisional delight in their intercourse, which could have been conducted better on a sunny day in Kinvara, or a wet freezing one for that matter, where no one would have been suffering from travel.

Yet, regardless of the difficulties, they were pleased enough. In particular, two of them, the most unexpected two. One was a savage little painter, who, unlike the others, looked younger than the catalogue photograph and who daubed colours in and out of and over each other in a way that no one could understand. She was here, either because she was a complete fraud or because she was a genius, the jury was out and probably could not be forced to reach a quorum anyway. The second was a seemingly surly, long novelist, who made people relax when he smiled, this because he had them otherwise so strained that the relief of seeing his teeth was aerobic.

The painter was taking time out to think of her life, as if that would smooth the edges of it, but in the meantime she was wondering how she would wash her clothes, and wishing she'd bought a travel iron in duty free. She laughed to herself a lot, not being used to overwhelming company, and tried not to light her cigarettes because her lighter, bought in duty free, had the letters I R E L A N D and an embarrassed shamrock emblazoned across it. Not a suitable accoutrement for a painter whose paintings could not be understood. The novelist wanted to get her to bed, not because he had an unfulfilled sexual appetite, in fact his libido was comfortably low, but because doing something that he'd heard other people did might help his next chapter.

Mary Ellen, for that was her name, and John James, for that was his, were to bump into each other a few times over the next ten days. The first time was in the bar, the arranged meeting place for those who were not God enough to be at the Big Dinner. He was speeding up his drinking in order to keep time with his inner fury; she was getting drunk because, although she knew better, she had become hypnotised into matching pace with him, in his race to oblivion. Nothing much was being said, and what was, was gauche enough, she thought. Mary Ellen explained to John James that she had once read a story about academics who were going to a conference that had no theme. Their orders were to address only what they didn't know.

'Do you ever write anything like that?'

He was disgusted.

'Not that I remember offhand.'

In the restaurant afterwards one of their number, who had

never eaten fondue, nearly got sick when the raw meat arrived at the table. Two Americans sat at the next table and loudly ordered tomato sandwiches and soda water, causing great relief because they could now discuss America, where the language had the same letters as their own but felt inferior in sentence; this would take the spotlight off the fondue virgin. As they left, a diner at another nearby table had steak tartare, and the weak-stomached poet had to be rushed out into the night air. Good night.

In her hotel room Mary Ellen opened a small bottle of champagne, thinking that it should be cheap, this being its country of origin. She did not read the tinily printed warning that placed its value at almost twenty pounds. Ignorance of this fact helped her to sleep, despite a roar of traffic that resembled back-to-back runways. She dreamt of what it was that needed to be smoothed. In the morning she washed her bra, pants and socks, and seeing them there lying side by side, bodiless, on the towel gave her great comfort. She ate her roll and jam grate-fully.

In John James's room he put on yesterday's clothes, and hated the smell of his hangover – it was alien, raced his heart, and he couldn't think how the next chapter could be started. He wasn't pleased any more, if he had ever been.

All the writers and painters and musicians left their various hotels and taxied or métroed to the round table at a book fair, where they would try to explain the unexplainable. But first they had to walk through millions of paperbacks and hard-backs, past determined publishers and nonchalant translators. They bumped into entourages that were trying to hide men in inner circles, as if there were a hundred Mike Tysons on the way to Appeals. The table was rectangular and dipped un-evenly, both on the surface and between the legs. The heat was foreign and made them cranky. They listened to their describers describing them, spoke their three minutes, some sprinkling inner reserves on their replies, one taking refuge in religion.

Mary Ellen started grappling with one definite thing that needed to be smoothed in her life, and had to be kicked under the table when it came her turn to speak. John James put his fury in wicked, staccato, low mutters and longed for a drink. When the half-born talk was wound up and put away disconsolately, they left the room, wondering if that had been what had shaken them from their rooms at home, dragged them out to airports and on to buses that shivered above the clouds. They separately escaped, but to where? They would say later on that evening that they had walked to *museés*, found second-hand book shops, or met long lost friends. And if, in truth, they couldn't have cared less if they'd never seen some of those friends this side of hell, this was not the place to say it.

On this second night they ate together more comfortably, the sight of home in view for some, those on short visits. They heaped their complaints together, making a mountain in the middle of the table, but not wishing to blame the wrong person. These things could be sieved and filtered into small annoyances in their respective houses, where food, work, the weather, school time and cranky neighbours would take priority. John James tried to contact Mary Ellen across a two foot barrier but she flitted from eye to eye, like a bus conductor, and squashed his every attempt mercilessly. Her ignorance of his intent was of the most crushing. He would never get the next chapter on its feet. Goodnights were said in staggers, reluctantly, that only because of a certain wakefulness. At last the final five were swallowed into taxis and their rooms. Mary Ellen's clothes were dry. She would leave the comfort of folding them for the ordinary task of the morning. À la Thomas Kinsella, she noticed that wrinkles were forging little paths on the soft part of her cheeks, a most peculiar place surely.

They had lunch together before scattering to places they didn't know, where they hoped they would be treated well, which might not be possible, because everyone's idea of being treated well is different. They were all out of this city today, spread like forks of lightening to far corners, except for Mary Ellen, who would have to spend one cold day foraging down wet streets, having given up the battle against cleaners and fridge refillers to sleep the afternoon away. She too was getting unpleased. Oh yes, and John James was there too, but he had behaved so strangely at lunch that Mary Ellen preferred to think of him as also gone. The exchange, like all others between them, had begun pointlessly enough.

'I don't like marmalade, isn't that interesting?' he said.

'Mm.'

'I said that I don't like marmalade. I like jams and sweet tastes and oranges but not marmalade, isn't that interesting?'

'Hm.'

She couldn't figure how to respond. She thought of colours. But novelists were probably terribly talky, so she thought she'd better say something.

'It's not particularly "interesting", it's a fact.'

'Really, you don't find it interesting?' he mimicked. 'It's a fact.'

One of the Northern Poets said, 'Oh come, it's neither interesting nor uninteresting. And it is a fact, or so you've told us. You know, they say that travel broadens the mind. Myself, I think it can narrow it.'

That got them off marmalade.

Later she lay in her bed, having forgotten her life, never mind what needed to be smoothed. John James threw his clothes into his bag. Everything was at the door ready for morning. He emptied the fridge of all the drink, a lethal mixture of taste and effect.

On his way, by taxi, to the airport he saw Mary Ellen trundling with her bags towards a metro mouth. She looked cold. He wished that he was able to talk like a normal man, a bit of nonsense, a little charm, some solid serious words that would spark a painter's interest. He waved from the taxi but she did not see him, wasn't looking out for him of course.

John James proceeded by plane to the next place, a small town that boasted an unexplained interest in visiting artists. He wound his way glumly through the first night county council speeches, thought of Mary Ellen, and decided to grow a beard. During the week, in bed at night, he also organised people's funerals, the music, the attendance, where to go afterwards, whether to have soup and sandwiches or a meal, before drinking the cold wet evening away, and how much to miss the recently deceased. It gave him something to do and seemed more spiritual than contemplating how he would spend the money if he won the lottery.

John James's minder was a peculiar nervous Englishwoman, who had only one interesting characteristic but it was all of her. She seemed fragile and frightened, yet she had walked away from a husband because he didn't like her poems. She showed them to John James; they were bad. On the third morning, the day after he had given a particularly uncoordinated reading, she brought him walking over the nearby hills. They had little to say to each other, but managed to match equal amounts of small talk so that there was not an uncomfortable block of silence. He was interested in watching her because she reminded him of someone and he hadn't yet figured out who it was. On the way home she brought him to meet Gil, a neighbour who had fled his luxurious past life and was now living as a recluse up the sort of lane that can be found in many places, in many countries – the kind of alley that gives comfort to those who can endure a large degree of pessimism without killing themselves. The man had been an intellectual star; he had been so busy that he didn't know that he was alive. New things had happened to him hourly and he had no idea what age he was. On a métro or underground somewhere, he saw a woman reading a profile of himself, must have been New York, it was in English, definitely English, and he hadn't been in London much that year. She was so engrossed in the article that when she accidentally kicked him she didn't even see him as she grudgingly apologised. The interruption had distracted her from this great article. Apparently that did it for him.

John James wondered whether to be sad, admiring or jealous. Gil's head rocked continuously as he spoke, mesmerising his listeners. He was now writing a book on Time and showed his only grin of the visit when John James asked how long he thought it would take. He invited them to stay for the evening meal but the minder was too uneasy in her sudden disinterest and so she said, 'We've arranged to meet one of the other Irish artists in the next town.'

The excuse limped into the atmosphere that was now clouded with the possibility that the recluse didn't like being alone. Gil left them to the car, having first kissed his faithful donkey, who stood near the door watching for movement and life.

'The donkey is bored, I think,' John James said, as they drove down the path.

'Women cannot afford the luxury of such arrogant negativity. If they allowed themselves to feel like that, they would never have children. And while I don't want them myself, I'm glad someone else does,' his minder said.

Her anger was surprising. So it hadn't been disinterest. And now he remembered who she was like, three people, actually. His first girlfriend, a waif of a thing from Belfast who now spent a lot of time hugging all sorts of people in the hope of bringing on a peace and who, coincidentally, also wrote bad poetry; a Scottish stage designer who had a notorious interest in other women's husbands; and a German pastry-maker who had taken him to bed once and declared him a failure. At this rate of memory he'd soon get the next chapter started. There would be no need for Mary Ellen.

'And who is the other Irish artist that we're going to meet?'

'Mary something.'

'Mary Ellen something?'

'That's right.'

Well, well, John James thought, she didn't tell me that she was coming up this way. It would be good to meet her, now that he was settled in his unsettledness and less grumpy.

Mary Ellen's week had been much the same as John James's. A flight out of Paris, towns blurring into one impression, cheerful sunny days ended by dry cold nights. She had spoken about her paintings, about colour, colour and Ireland. Everything seemed to have 'and Ireland' tagged on, which was a good and a bad thing. She preferred to separate the two discussions, because certainly she never thought of Ireland, of being Irish, when she mixed her palette. On her last night she went for a meal with a dozen or so men and women, all of whom were probably interesting and worth remembering, but the concerto of beautiful foods and wines won attention so completely that all those people would fade into one amorphous being, that was there on that night at that table. She was looking forward to meeting that novelist John James the next night.

He said, 'Hello, did you have a good time?' And soon they were comfortably in conversation, excited at their common wonders. John James's guide was also relieved, glad to be able to glide through her own new language with her acquaintances in the small bar. She was relieved at being able to speed up her sentences. John James and Mary Ellen compared their past CVs – the hotel work, cleaning toilets, mortuary sluice downing. Not wanting to get depressed, they only skirted talk of the money their friends were making. They had a moment's silence in honour of what might have been if they hadn't both volunteered to be held ransom to an idea. Ideas. What could John James say to her that might shift their conversation to intimacy. 'Come here to me' might do just as well as something more sophisticated. No, he would leave it, for the moment anyway. Ideas, that was a better place for the two of them. Sometimes risk was a good thing, even if it brought disaster. Disaster could be interesting, shift the lethargy out of a day. But then there would be all that palpitation. Not tonight.

Later, in her room, Mary Ellen counted the quarter hours until it would be late enough to go to bed. She ran too fast from the toilet to hear the Sky News headlines, even though she knew that they would be back on again in thirty minutes. She should not have been so discontent, surely she should have been glad to be out of her country, to have time to relegate her worries to a background, in a way that was only possible far from home. She was a little glad, but hadn't managed to reach a level of disconnection that would allow her to let things happen to her as if she was an unmade individual, a pre-person.

In John James's room he wondered why vague unhappiness suited him. Perhaps it kept him safe, and this was an important thing, because he came from an accident-prone family.

At breakfast they were told that a small plane had crashed at dawn into the rocks beside their guest house. Over there, a mile or so away. And no one had heard a sound. Mary Ellen, who often dreamt of seeing a plane crash, could not believe that no one had heard a sound. In her dreams it was always the noise that alerted people to the sight, before the ball of fire dazzled them and the bodies began to rain from the sky. It was this kind of picture that made it hard for her to behave herself like an adult on aeroplanes. She asked John James if he would walk with her to the plane, not because she wanted to be a voyeur, but because she thought that, given this opportunity, she should try to see if she could imagine whether death was indeed different this way.

As they walked to the scene they passed cursory glances over the vegetation – that might be the thousand-year-old juniper tree which was reputed to bring luck, that was thyme, and look at the wild asparagus. Mary Ellen wanted to see the wreckage quickly, now unsure if she was doing the right thing. And then she saw it, a plane all right, scarred by the impact of this rocky hard half-mountain. What a place to die. Although the bodies had been carried away hours ago, the presence of the three people, one woman and two men, was definite, loud almost. Some clothes were still scattered about. Jeans, white shirts. Mary Ellen imagined the clothes they were wearing and red polo necks came to mind a lot, which must be unlikely, considering that the plane had started its journey in Tunisia or Tangiers, or somewhere beginning with a T that was hot. Would you choose different clothes if you knew that you were going to die in them rather than merely cover yourself with them for the day? And then there was the smell. She couldn't compare it to anything, but it was there. Indeed, this might well be the smell of energy leaving the body, of spirits burning out.

The plane was small, but not completely wrecked. There was still an enclosed space where someone could have survived, but not today, the luck was out. Littered over the side of the hill were cigarette butts, hundreds and hundreds of them, someone never cleaned their ashtrays. And maps, maps

of the earth not the skies. Had they been looking at them –
'See, there we are' – when they began to rush towards that
dot on the map where they were to part from their bodies,
and, yes, it was on that page, because every place has a dot on
a map. And sugar lumps. Again hundreds upon hundreds of
sugar lumps. Ordinary sugar lumps. At least one could pre-
sume that they were ordinary, wouldn't the gendarmes have
been here, wouldn't they have taken them away if they'd
thought they weren't ordinary sugar lumps, aren't the gendarmes always right? Perhaps one of the dead people had a
friend who loved sugar lumps and as a joke, they had bought
a box as a present. They were all the same brand, if they had
been different then perhaps one of the passengers had a fetish
about collecting sugar lumps in cafés, restaurants and bars. Perhaps all year the collector's family used the various and varied
sugar lumps of travel? No, they were all the same brand. A
yellow scarf, with sparkling gold threads glinting through it,
flapped about on a thorny bush, making the slapping noise of
washing on a clothesline. That would belong to the woman.
Or maybe not, these men were from North Africa, where
colour is not anathema to males and they wear sprigs of
jasmine behind their ears.

Mary Ellen wished that she could pray, it seemed wrong not
to speed the spirits away from this white barren hill of stones. It
was improper that she and John James were here instead of
their friends or family. The two men and one woman had
not yet become statistics in a death notice, they were with
them as if risen from the dead, sorry that it was these two strangers who were here, not someone who knew them and almost
all about them.

Mary Ellen had wanted to stand in the spot, not to wonder
what was in the minds of the passengers, but to feel if the
nightmare left a mark. Dying, she presumed, was bad enough,

it must be a falling, so dying flying would be death in stereo. Still, it seemed not that bad really, an ordinary end, the wind would have fanned their private thoughts, consoled their worries. It was simply a place of death like any other, an outdoor spot for expiry. John James held out his hand. They each closed their fingers around the other's and dreamt the spirits back for a moment to say a proper, if inadequate, goodbye. Would this man do to lead her through a tragedy? Perhaps this was why they had come on the tour, not to represent anything but to meet, to be here, to find out that there could be no easy coming together, that things are harder than that, that everything can't have a light-hearted corridor, which when quickly passed through will lead to intimacy.

They tiptoed away from the scene and felt it appropriate to have a small drink. The next morning they gratefully boarded a bus. As it rounded a hairpin bend Mary Ellen drew her breath in loudly; there was the scrunched-up plane thrown over the side of the hill, dumped as a crashed car might be, no effort made to bury it away from sudden sight.

'The place where a plane crashes is just a place like any other, no particular colour. I suppose you can prepare yourself for death quickly, you will have done many preparations unknown to yourself,' Mary Ellen said.

'Comic poets, or novelists for that matter, get warmth during their lifetimes, which can be no unenjoyable thing, but the serious will be remembered, if only by a few,' John James said, as if it was a reply.

He never wanted sex anyway, he preferred gardening and growing tomatoes.

ACCORDING TO MICHAEL

Once upon a time – that is, last year – two women drank coffee in Bewley's of Grafton Street, and tried to talk everything off three years, tried to hint things together chronologicaily, to overview events, to swim people and their actions and their intentions in and out of the stream. Gossip, it's called. They did this because it said their lives out to each other and thus made them seem more understandable.

There had been a long six months, fifteen years before, when they had come here every Saturday, them and their pleased crowd. They had eaten small breakfasts, had lots of coffee and cinnamon buns. They had read their copies of the *Irish Times* and been widely envied because everyone could see that they were it that year. A small group of lucky people who could have been the cloud in *Les Idées Claires* – Michael would have said that, he was the only art student in their crowd. They rarely understood his references, but never gave up pretending that they had.

But the stone moved on top of them and in some cases hit off the cloud. There was tragedy and failure, as well as contentment and dizzy success. The most unexpected rose to the top, the most unexpected slid to the bottom. Some of them married others of them, some of the women married farmers.

(No fear of that for our two in Bewley's, they were farmers' daughters and knew better.) Some married and separated with indecent, suspicious haste; some lingered through years. Many emigrated and added that particular sweet and sourness to their lives. Barbara was one of those, now living in Boston.

'I'm glad it's all over,' Barbara said, referring to sexual desire, 'it was a thing that could drive you mad.' She said she hadn't felt an urge, an uncontrollable one, for more than a year.

'And what did you do if it was uncontrollable?' Sadhbh asked.

'Mostly,' she said, 'I went to pubs or nightclubs, got drunk, very drunk, and found a man.'

'Why did you have to get drunk?' Sadhbh asked, thinking what a waste of sensation. She bolstered the unfairness of her question with a tone of patronisation that was really born of envy.

'If a woman who needs it has not been asked by the second drink, she'll get drunk for sure. And then she can ask herself.'

'With all your degrees in sociology?'

'Those never helped get a man on a dark night,' Barbara said.

But that wasn't what Sadhbh had meant. Sadhbh had meant, why would Barbara get so drunk at all, having all those degrees, masters actually?

Barbara and Sadhbh were different, as most people are. They come, or came, from the same place, a village in County Monaghan. In Ireland you always come from your county even if it be only so many miles by so few. But some people get to say *came* from. They met and maybe loved each other because of this geography. In fact, it was the coming-fromness that made them meet, the love was luck and icing.

'Anyway, it's all over now, thank God. That inconvenient hunger has been fed. I hope. What about you?'

'I've never really not enjoyed sex. I think I've been lucky,' Sadhbh said, dodging the truth. And she recounted how she'd met her husband and reminded herself and Barbara how placid and almost great her life was, which was a little petty, considering everything Barbara had just told her. And untrue.

But she reminded herself later that these three-yearly conversations with holidaying emigrants were too difficult because they raked up comatose and dangerous feelings which were best left hidden. Feelings that were as things which Sadhbh had been looking after, hoping that no one would come back to pick them up. Of course her reply had been only half-honest, not because it was half-dishonest but because it was wholly half-honest. She had, after all, shut down the truth. It was not something that she liked talking about. Anyway, sex and everything with it, love, flirting even, had always come as surprises to her, as extras, so it was easy to trim her expectations.

In wintertime when Sadhbh was young she had never thought that she wouldn't always have to play cards with the old ones at home, while her brothers went to dances or just went out. Out where? Out into the dark lane? Or out down the road? But there's nothing down the road. Dances – maybe she could understand that, although she couldn't fit an interest in dancing with her big lolloping brothers. Here she was very wrong. Unlike most, they were not going to dances merely to see people, they were in fact the best jivers for miles around. They spun their troubles into handleable disappointment in perfectly timed circles.

Then one evening she was told that she could go with them. Luckily, she too had rhythm, so was no disgrace on the floor and never experienced wall-flowering. Well, once or twice, but she assumed that this travesty had happened only because someone hadn't got to her on time or hadn't seen her before asking someone else.

A few months later she went to the pictures with a man. She had never been before, the nearest picture house being ten miles away. The darkness shocked her, but that was soon to be nothing. The man put his arm on her shoulders. Casually, loosely. It took Sadhbh all of a long quarter minute to realise what the weight was. It was so dark she thought that something might have fallen on her shoulder. When the truth dawned on her a type of nausea, never before experienced, came over her body, her stomach sprouted troughs and she thought she would faint. The man must have felt the rigor because he excused himself. While he was gone she wondered should she run away, but how would she get home? She knew no one in this town. She didn't even know the road out of it. He came back with a box of Roses and didn't put his arm near her again. She would have liked to eat one of the chocolates in gratitude, but her tongue was stuck to the roof of her mouth and stayed there for hours even after he had left her home, even after she had thrown the chocolates into the stove. The poor man. Never had such hatred been felt for such a small gesture.

Sadhbh protected herself from privatised encounters with boys for a long time after that, but then, mysteriously, she became ready, and fell into casual dating with a boy who was the same age as herself. Her first kiss was a surprise rather than a thrill, the second was distasteful, the third was more than satisfactory. In time the two of them negotiated a lying down beside each other in a field, and she had an astonishing clothes-on, little-touch, just-weight orgasm. Thus did the geography of her sexual life begin.

'Sadhbh Quinn, find the source of the river, and trace it to its outlet.'

'Yes, miss.'

'No, the Shannon does not start in Limerick, it starts in Sliabh Cuilcagh in Cavan, it ends in Limerick. There's a difference between a beginning and an ending. You know that, Sadhbh, I presume?'

Indeed she did. She was well acquainted with the ending – the ending of life, with its inevitability, its importance, indeed there was a continuous effort being made to make sure that she never forgot it, and prepared herself for it well. Why, only last month Mickey Larmer and James Linden had crashed into each other going around a corner. James Linden shouldn't really have been on their road because it could hold only one car, he should have taken the main road. It was so close. The rosary beads in Mickey Larmer's pocket were crushed and there wasn't a scratch on him. He could have been killed. He should have been killed, they said, their voices rising hysterically. Sadhbh exchanged 'nearly was' for 'should' in order to get to the root of the hysteria. And they marvelled at how two cars would just happen to meet on a blind corner, exactly when the hedges had overgrown wildly, the holes in them casting bright shadows across the road, so bright they would take the sight away from anyone's eyes. And how, when that did happen nothing more serious had to be done than mend the doors, put a lick of paint on them and buy a new pair of rosary beads. Oh yes! You had to stay on the side of God.

'How does the source of a river begin? Does it start with a drop of rain or what, miss? And why does the river go one way and not another and why does a mountain rise up where it does and how come?'

'You'll learn all of those details in time, Sadhbh.'

Sadhbh's father and mother taught her about the evil of sex through a series of verbal contortions, intakings of breath and loud aggravating sighs. They laid down markers so that

Sadhbh knew, without being specifically told, that she was not to go near the New Houses, a county council estate at the end of the village, where the sexual habits were less rigid than out their road. So who did Sadhbh first really and truly love? A man from the New Houses, of course. But they got her to Dublin to a university just in the nick of time, where God-alone-knew who she'd meet. All they could do was hope.

During the Bewley's six months Michael asked her to marry him and she told him not to be so silly. She had neither the broad view nor age to help her answer the question in a real way. She told him that you couldn't just ask someone to marry you. Michael persisted and said that you could, because you had to start somewhere and there wasn't an infinite number of questions that a person could put before getting down to the important one. But it dawned on Michael, slowly, that Sadhbh had really refused him, that she wasn't simply playing the coquette. He had vaguely heard of Mount Isa, Queensland, once, and thought that that should be far enough away.

'I won't be distracted by art galleries there,' he told Sadhbh, and said that he'd always wanted to go to a mining town, hadn't he told her? When he was gone a few weeks Sadhbh realised that there is more to a map than the co-loured-in mountains. That summer she didn't notice the trees dressing up, or the flowers pollinating all over the place, or the sun showing off. She became acquainted with the feeling of feeling.

In time, that being a word that gives some notion of Sadhbh's sense of loss, she married. Her flatmate, Barbara in fact, had convinced her to try wearing a pair of false eyelashes as they dressed for their Saturday night out. Perhaps it was the unexpected heat in the pub corner or maybe she hadn't used the solution properly, whatever, a sensation made itself known to her, that of roof tiles tumbling irresistibly towards the ground. A person can think a lot in a moment like that and Sadhbh saw a woman's pants, at one of the home dances, creep down her legs. The woman had stepped seriously out of them and kicked them under a seat in perfect time. So Sadhbh caught the offending eyelash before it fell into her Guinness, ripped the other one off and popped both of them into her matchbox without missing a beat of her conversation. The man who was listening to her felt a great joy squeeze into his bones. He had to marry her, and because Sadhbh didn't know how to refuse twice, they did.

Time was spent, children were born, holidays were had, letters were written, Barbara and others were seen when they came home.

Sadhbh now told Barbara that she had not intended to see Michael on his first visit back. She had met him accidentally. She was running in and out of late night Thursday shops too busily when she felt the heat of someone looking at her. When she realised that it was Michael who was stepping towards her, with his mouth slightly open, she blinked. Her stomach blushed. They kissed quickly on the cheeks. Observant passers-by would have smelt singeing. After ticking off the luggage of their lives, small inconsequential things, like spouses, offspring, addresses, wages for bread, they made a casual arrangement to have coffee at ten o'clock on Saturday morning. Both of them tried their best to weigh the words with ordinariness, but puffs of tunes came into the sentences, making a sudden untraceable music heard above the street din. Some people looked around, then told themselves that they had only imagined it.

And when that Saturday had happened, when its creation of intimacies had exploded into dusk, the pasts of Michael and

Sadhbh had been bloodily stained with unfillable desire. The mistake of finding out would be with them for ever.

Michael returned to Australia on Sunday. Sadhbh was sorry that she knew that. She listened for the noise of every plane in the sky.

Since then there was only one certainty. After all the building of a life, she now knew that there was nothing propping it up inside. Every daily task became a falsehood, but most of all, sex and everything leading to it became a colossal lie. Her husband, who had never done her any harm, seemed to be a torturer. His hands, that were only hands, became objects of fear, his skin became as thorns and she dared not think of his penis because of the terror it held. All bad. All that geography dried up. Memory become an enemy.

'How long ago did this happen, who have you told?' Barbara asked sadly, when Sadhbh had finally wound herself out to the end of her story.

'Two years. No one.'

'Is there nothing you can do?'

'I remember Michael saying that, unlike Rodin, we can't divide the body into sections and make them pretend that they have nothing to do with each other.'

'He would,' Barbara implied.

'What?'

'Nothing.'

'I thought I should tell someone. I thought that saying it might make it not be true. I thought that if I told you it might make it easier.'

'And has it?'

'I'll see.'

Barbara wondered if the weight of such a thing could flatten a person, could drag them slowly, prematurely, into the earth.

Sadhbh dropped Barbara, on her way back to Boston, out to the airport. Barbara said, 'I'll call you, sorry ring you, at Christmas.'

In reply, Sadhbh said, 'An awful lot of planes leave here every day. Go places.'

THE UNDEATHING OF GERTRUDE

There was Betty, a face so fragile it might disappear before you as if it hadn't been coloured in. And Tim, he could wipe that sorrowful look off his face, he would get a woman – old men might say more fool she, surely no one could marry that cheap, and they would know that what she was marrying him for wouldn't last – still he would get a woman. And Mary, ragged-looking as a crooked road, always pretending to think about one of her children, but that was bluffing; she couldn't bear to think of her mother and father, that's why she wore her maternal look. And James, home from America, twitching to get back to his plastic life, where to own was to understand. Well, it's good that Gertrude hadn't died after all.

The children hung around for a few days, generally getting on his nerves as they swayed about the place, having long tele-phone conversations with their friends, explaining over and over again how their mother had died and her not dead at all. When they left, he and Gertrude sighed with relief.

Eddie McGivern got thin gradually. He had to be careful, you see, because his neighbours, as well as his children, believed that his wife was dead, so he was forced to buy food for only one and then share it with Gertrude. As she had always been a very healthy eater, this meant that even less than half of what he bought went into his own mouth.

The shopkeeper in the village told the next-door neighbour, as they discussed him in doubtful voices, that he seemed to be doing grand, he hadn't lost his appetite or anything like that, judging by his purchases. Still, he was getting thin and no doubt about it. The neighbour said, yes, indeed, he could vouch for the appetite because he had called many mornings and he was having two boiled eggs for his breakfast, two, that was a thing he could never do himself, have more than one boiled egg.

The mornings the neighbour called were indeed the days on which Eddie and Gertrude had boiled eggs – the unfortunate thing was that Eddie could have an egg only one half the number of times, because that shopkeeper was so nosy she would twig that there was something up if he was still buying the same amount of eggs that they had always bought before people said that Gertrude had died. The same with bread, butter, milk, bacon – everything in fact.

Eddie McGivern was a different kind of man. When he first met Gertrude he brought her out for meals occasionally, which was not normal at the time – people ate in in those days, they didn't talk about food – and asked her how was that and was the dessert nice. They went for long walks, both of them very interested in scenery. They exhausted themselves describing it to each other, taking private pleasure out of what their descriptions actually meant – look at that hollow in the tree, you can put your hand in it; this valley is always wet. Perhaps they were before their time. Eddie knew people who had to beg guests to come to their wedding. Not Gertrude. People wanted to visit them even years after they got married. Gertrude was a navigator – when she didn't know things, she felt them; he was a born pilot – he wasn't afraid to start anything. As they got older they didn't always finish their own sentences

– sometimes they finished them for each other, sometimes they didn't bother. They lived together so long it was not a matter any more of love or hate. Of course, they hated each other sometimes, as is right for mature people. They still, even after people supposed her dead, had rows, naturally. On the days when he had a row with Gertrude he got into very bad form, really bad form. He knew that the neighbour noticed these moods but he never told him what caused them.

The summer after people said that Gertrude died, James came home from America. All the children came down and insisted on visiting the family grave. Eddie had a bit of an argument with Gertrude that morning because she said that for their sakes he should go, it would keep them happy, and he didn't see why he should have to, he hated graveyards. In the end she won. So there he was, caught among all these graves. No matter which way he turned they were there, rushing towards him like a bush fire. The children had put a railing around the grave as if someone was trying to get out. Well, if they were, the children were putting a stop to it. They had also put grotesque toys on top of it, plastic flowers and the like. Tim wandered around the graveyard reading aloud ancient headstones. He liked visiting old things. Pity, then, he didn't come home a bit more often, you'd think for his mother's sake he could try.

The children thought that Eddie was not coping well, he was distant and sometimes lapsed into conversation with himself, he was also getting very thin. They needled him so much about sitting around the place twiddling his thumbs that he decided he would soon show them. Next week.

Eddie cleared out the old garage and put a door on it. He had to put the door on in order to stop the neighbours from seeing what he was doing. He drove to Dundalk, where he bought all he needed. Then he set to showing the children just how busy he could make himself. He would paint Gertrude's and his life right up to this day. The board was twenty feet long and three feet deep, so there should be enough room.

He pencilled in the important dates first, making sure to leave the right amount of space between them. He hammered or stuck on symbols, mainly to use up space and to save him painting the entire board. He was not, after all, a real painter, so he needed guidelines as well as secret reminders. He put a sprig of hawthorn bush in the year they had built the house, hawthorn because it was steady. He put a piece of candle at the end of each year, that was for soft lights at Christmas and love so unbearable at times it might explode but it didn't, it just seeped out in touches and small things done for each other. They lit a candle in the window every Christmas Eve night before they left for midnight mass and pulled the curtains well back so they wouldn't catch fire. When they got electricity they simply switched on the lights. The light, that first Christmas, because Gertrude thought one light in the kitchen was enough, they would not need bulbs in the bedrooms, but she changed her mind six months later. In the morning at early mass the frost sparkled like diamonds in the ground, the squeal of the bagpipe band starting up sent shivers down their backs.

He began at the top left-hand corner, painting a small boy and girl. The boy had his finger in his mouth more from contemplation than from fear, because he didn't know yet that there were things to fear. The girl was in her grandmother's house. After debts had been satisfied she was finally housed in an outhouse that had been a stable for stallions. The children thought it great fun until they discovered that they were going to live there. For real. The girl had her finger in her mouth but it meant a different thing. It was a pity that her children hated her, considering all this.

Eddie painted Gertrude at points in her life, he painted her every six inches or so, sometimes three inches from the top of the board, sometimes sitting, sometimes bending, sometimes at an angle. He painted her from above, climbed a ladder and painted her from her feet upwards, concentrating on her arms flung up, which looked different from there than if he had been standing in front of her. It was as if he was on a balcony watching a dancer down below. Gertrude was a great dancer.

As her years and the painting progressed she grew fatter and more comfortable. In dreams he painted himself beside her. Their bodies ran into each other in circles, head to toe, toe to head, head to toe, on and on into infinity like a hula hoop. They looked sometimes like musical notes. There were moments when his portrait stood back from hers, baffled. When she was having babies, when she was feeding babies, when she was sick with exhaustion, when she was plain sick, the only thing he could do for her was to think about her and that's a fact. He couldn't talk to her or mind her, he could only think of her. He explained this in letters to her. He was writing letters to her now, asking her questions about little things that he couldn't remember. He was writing to her for two reasons: first, because she sometimes went away these days and was hard to contact, and second, it was easier to get all the questions down in a letter. He explained why he could only think of her, not mind her, when she was sick, why he had to occasionally drop out of their lives together, in case he learned too much. He told her that when she had first loved him he had walked around dazed – how could she love him? He told her that loving her had purified him.

Eddie had difficulty with colours. He had thought it would be so easy. His brushes were no good either. Earlier, the rasping of the jagged edge of his big brush had been the right sound and had made the right marks. But that was during the rough work – he had even used Gertrude's old turkey wing,

her soot brush, then. He had used it to scratch the paint between the trees, to make them less dense because it was not true
that they couldn't see out through them in the summertime.
Light changes always got to their back door. The trees were
hard though. They nearly sent him demented. He had to go
out to them again and again to watch them, to take them in,
because he couldn't paint outside. The neighbours. Just as well,
the weather would never have held up.

Eddie was also having difficulty getting the depth, not the
depth, but how deep it was, how far back, how far in. He
could see it when he looked at it face-on, but it wasn't coming
out right. This would not have hurt so much if he had not
known the depth. He would take a break, go visit Mary, buy
new brushes. In Dublin they might know something about
how to mix colours.

Mary was all tense, like a top ready for spinning. How she
could have got like that he couldn't imagine. He remembered
trying to get her to say *ant* instead of *pismire*, but no, she was
too full of life for that. Mary was determined not to be
dragged down by what must be interminable grief – her
parents had got on so well, she couldn't bear to think about it.
Although how anyone could have got on so well with either
of them, she didn't know. Still, he seemed remarkably well.
Mentally, not physically. Like Betty. She used 'in June' for
shorthand instead of saying 'when Mother died', or else she
said 'that time Mother died' as if it had been a once off thing
and had not stayed happened.

Eddie talked and talked as if words were worth nothing.
Mary scrubbed and scrubbed, so she might not hear them all.
Eddie remembered the evening he gave her the paper with
Campbell's auction in it, when she was a child: 'Read that out
till we hear how good you are.' She read, 'A large farmhouse
with water nearby and a lot of nice ties.' 'Niceties,' Eddie

corrected her. She smiled, always pleasant while taking correction, not like the others. Gertrude beamed at them. Gertrude had furrows around her eyes from all the beaming she did.

Now Mary was scrubbing wildly to shut out the sound of his voice. She was afraid it would steal away her next decade or two and she hadn't got decades to play with. When he tried to link her for help crossing the busy roads, her arm froze as if he was attacking her. But Eddie had told her that it was all right to believe that snow is blue. 'It looks blue, I can see,' he said. 'Something to do with the light.' He had told her that the stars were lamps in the sky to guide us and that clusters of stars were countries in the sky. She scrubbed harder and harder.

Eddie and Mary walked out to the shops in Donnybrook.

'That's the house they cut in half to widen the road, isn't it?' he said.

Mary said, 'Yes', sharply.

'Imagine, their kitchen would have been here,' he tapped his foot on the path.

Mary sighed and hurried him on. She thought that herself every time she passed the house, but she couldn't afford to let him in on her life. If he had someone at home, that would be different. She was beginning to perspire heavily. He wanted to buy socks. She, for no reason, bought a pair of satin knickers with imitation pearls on them. If she hadn't bought them, she might have been sucked in by him. The sides of the knickers were cut out and the pearls were sewn around the edges in a triangle where the pubic hair would be. She would never wear them. Still, it didn't matter, it had put him in his place for a while, shut him up. Eddie thought that if she was buying stuff like that, maybe she wasn't as far gone as he had imagined. Mary left him in the hardware shop. He insisted that she go on home; he would be back in half an hour.

Mary's youngest said, 'That's the pits.'

'Do you know what that means?' Eddie asked.

'It means "awful",' the child said.

'When the children in the workhouses had to dig their own graves in the very flowerbeds they had planted, there were so many graves the flowerbeds had to be used too, that was called "digging the pits". I think.'

Mary swung around. 'There's no need to frighten the child.'

'I didn't mean . . .'

In bed that night Mary said to her husband, 'My father showed me the sun dancing at the top of the ploughed field every Easter Sunday. He held a mirror to the light and showed me the sun dancing. I believed him. It was the reflection of bits of broken glass in the mirror but it doesn't matter. It was lovely believing him. Do you know what else he told us? That Jesus got away?' She finally went to sleep, determined to be gentler with her father but knowing that she wouldn't succeed.

Eddie went home, the hollow bit in the middle of him feeling bigger. He looked at his painting. He knew what he wanted it to be but he couldn't get it there. No matter how he pushed and cajoled, it didn't show. The Last Day, he had it pencilled in, Gertrude and he were there together. He hoped the Last Day didn't start too early, because Gertrude was never good in the mornings. The two of them hoped that all the neighbours would not be there. A person should be able to see that hope on their faces. But how could he, who was not a painter, paint a life? He was as exhausted as a drizzle trying to fill a bucket.

The auctioneer wrung his hands and told Mary that there was nothing he could have done about it. Eddie had come to him and asked that the contents of the house be sold. Only the contents. The neighbours turned up, either to buy, to stand beside him in this sad hour, or to nose about. Some of them would have been wondering about the house. The first three items were sold (the auctioneer said he knew who had them and they were willing to give them back), when Eddie started to bid himself. It was a delph ornament, a bird that once had a clock in it. Eddie said to Seamus Patterson beside him that it belonged to Gertrude and that she had told him to buy it back for her. Painters often did that, he said – went to auctions and bought back their own paintings. He bid on every second item, the neighbours bid against him all right because it would have looked odd if they hadn't. Her father had signed a cheque, the auctioneer had it right here, he hadn't cashed it, naturally. Her father hadn't taken the purchases with him either, just left and hadn't been seen since.

Mary thought the saddest part was the painting. She thought the bits that were finished were good and by the look of the pencilled scenes, he knew what he was doing. Betty and Tim were devastated. They searched the roads and odd little lanes months after everyone else had given up. In the end they concentrated only on the roads between Ballintra and Dundalk. He had definitely been there recently according to the paint receipts. People think that these roads are going somewhere, that they are even a chart and mean something. This is not true. They're just an absolute mess of pointless lanes going nowhere, just there to confuse people who have lost one or both of their parents. Poor Betty, poor Tim. Betty hears voices at night talking to each other. James didn't come home because there wasn't much point, was there?

At night Mary tells her children that Jesus got away.

TWO GOOD TIMES

'Let's have a good time,' Constance Holland said to an old flame, as if it could be ordered. Two good times, an insurance policy against them going wrong, and I'll have the change in notes. She was thirty-five and had grown up into a woman with sharp taste but with the nerve to go trashy sometimes. She could be a smart-arse in her imagination, but at home she scrubbed saucepans just like everyone else. And let the seriousness of life overcome the flippancy that sometimes flashed in her eyes.

'What would you like to drink?' her old flame, Gregory Duffy, asked.

'A bottle of good Australian red wine.'

'A bottle?' he queried, trying to keep surprise tucked away behind his voice.

'Oh yes, a bottle. There's no hurry on us, is there?'

'No, there's no hurry on us,' he chuckled, his surprise relievedly under control. A man could slip disastrously on the wrong note in a chance meeting like this. Not quite chance. But that was for him to know and her to find out. Perhaps.

Constance found a table and watched Gregory's back as he negotiated the drinks. There was some dealing to be done because the barman normally served wine only by the glass. Also,

Gregory was in a bit of a dither about what he would drink himself. Pints of lager might look pale beside the wine, especially if the last ray of the evening sun spurted through the stained glass window and coloured the wine mauve. His back was straight, still straight. She could see the side of his face. The confidence of time had ripened his look comfortably, the thinning of his hair had made his eyes bigger and clearer.

Fifteen months ago they had gone to Australia together. They had prepared as if this were not an undertaking, as if it was a normal journey to take. They had been companionable over packing suitcases, which certainly didn't feel normal to Constance. The companionability, that is. The aeroplane crept at a snail's pace across their individual television screens. It would have been a mesmerising thing to watch only the progress of that line. It could ultimately have driven them mad. Below them the lands of Europe ceded to Asia, the plane took a gentle right at Delhi and moved southeast, over the Bay of Bengal and eventually Malaysia. Most of the passengers were asleep when Darwin was crossed. But the whiff of it woke a few of them and they shyly made their ways to the back windows to stare down in wonder at empty dried rivers, the orange earth and silence. Constance had woken Gregory so that he could have a look, 'No rush though, there's hours of it yet before we get there.'

During their first week in Sydney, Constance could not take her eyes off the harbour. She wanted to prove something. Over the years when they and mutual friends had criss-crossed at parties, or more particularly at funerals, where one is apt to muse about other lives in other places, she had maintained that Sydney harbour was the most beautiful place in the entire world. Others had plumped for Paris, San Francisco, Moscow, the west of Ireland, even with the rain. Copenhagen, the architect amongst them always said.

'And anyway, how do you know about Sydney, you have never been there?'

'Not in this life.'

Gregory had believed her, without knowing it himself. That's why he had agreed to go. Now he too knew it. They had found a hotel so near the bridge it was almost on it. The bottom pane of the third-floor room showed water, the middle had trains running through it, and in the top pane she could view the walkers who were climbing over the arch. Lines of them, wearing convict uniforms, were tied together for safety reasons. They clip-clanged in shuffles, the occasional one catching her eye. She couldn't bear to draw the curtains, even when undressing.

Constance and Gregory opted for the walk across rather than up over. The bones in her body got light. Lost for words, they smiled at each other a lot, infected by their separate joys.

'Wouldn't it be perfect if time stopped here? I think I'm a pantheist,' she said.

'Are buildings and bridges part of this doctrine?'

'These ones are. But if I saw this every day, it would make me sad.'

'Why?'

'Because I would want to live for ever.'

They shivered together in the sun.

And then they had driven. Long long journeys. They watched the sun rise over Nambucca Heads, drank coffee and smoked cigarettes as the fishermen got out of their cars, wiped the sleep from their faces, and pushed their boats out. They shared the driving, saying the names out loud without comment. Narrandera, Dubbo, Winton, Goondiwindi. They stopped in a mining town, where miners fought with the insides of the earth. They agreed that lounging around this town was incongruous, the place was for work. The red of the earth was about minerals. Constance's need to marvel at its colour could get out of place. They took the road out to Cloncurry, leaving behind an army of ants, who sang over the sound of underground blasting. On the road again, she occasionally became aggravated by the insects. In Dublin, every June, she welcomed the first bluebottle into her home, cheered that its ugly buzzing and noisy life might mean that heat was on its way.

Tumbleweed tripped out over the roads on its unfathomable journey. When the kangaroo- and wallaby-watching became too much for them they pulled into clean-sheeted motels. They were swallowed by globes of sunsets every evening. And every morning saw them on the straight road again. They got excited when bends came up. They tried not to feel grief about strewn dead kangaroos, the ones who had not accomplished the last light jump into the bush.

In Coonabarabran, Constance bought a fiery opal. An Aboriginal woman painted adult bandicoots dropping their babies into the throat of a hollow log in order to save them from the burns of the first fire. She said that she was owned by the land. In Jerilderee, Gregory said, 'We could stay here.'

'For ever?'

'Why not?'

'Just leave everything and not go back. Our jobs and all?'

'Yes. And get up every morning to that sky.'

She looked up and was beginning to give it serious consideration, when he said, 'I suppose not.' Pity, she thought.

That evening the big news was about the apology. One side said that past injustice must be faced, that the word would clear the decks. The other worried secretly that all those Aborigines, who had kept the outback stations going with their cheap labour, and all those children stolen from home would be looking for compo. The only thing these people said out loud was that this generation should not have to apologise for something they didn't do. It would be enough to express regret. The two sides squared up to the word. It would be a long row. Constance and Gregory continued to call out names from the map.

On their last evening they asked directions to the restaurant where they had booked a table. The Scotsman wanted to tell his life to her. He loved the sound of her voice.

'When are you going back?'

'Tomorrow.'

'God.'

It felt rude to intrude on the grief of his longing − she would find the restaurant some other way.

'He was making a pass at you.'

'Don't be ridiculous, it was only homesickness.'

They had fish to eat. Tomorrow they would take the plunge into the morning of their leaving.

By the time they trooped on to the plane for the return journey, the single grey hair in her head had turned black again.

When they arrived home something happened. That's what Constance said when people asked, 'Where is Gregory?' She found it difficult to be grateful for the good things of her life, her decent history job, a place to live with trees growing outside it, friends who loved talking, no children to rear, little penny-watching to be done. She missed the brightness, the plants, the peculiar animals, the wild wild bird sound. She longed for the infinite distance. She became sad, went to bed early and examined her diary continuously, as if she had lost something of the future.

'It's not you,' she said, 'it's me.'

Wearied by her stoic mournfulness, Gregory took off to a new job in Cork, where he collected a whole bunch of new acquaintances and enjoyed his Australian, and other, memories in peace.

'Something happened,' she still said to her friends.

They asked Gregory.

'These things happen,' he said.

They gave up asking.

Constance looked at him now. He'd got the bottle of wine. A Dreamtime story says that a crater is caused by two stars dropping a child. Morning and Night are the parents still looking for the baby. The story lasts. She should know that, she had a history job. Time is such a small thing. Gregory was not after all, such a past flame. There was no time limit on their palms rubbing off each other's. (He would be glad to know that.)

'Make it two of those glasses, I'll have wine too,' he said.

And as he reached the table, the sun did slice through the stained glass window, lighting up their faces with a colour called glad.

ON THE INSIDE OF CARS

It was the beginning of a long weekend, and long weekends can be lonely, or good, or dangerous. The children were going by sea with their father to visit their paternal grandparents.

Chrissie got up early to do dreadful things, commit sacrifices to an image that she had never wanted. But she would prove to them that she could have children with polished shoes and matching clothes. Before she woke them she had early morning sickness not only from too little sleep, too many cigarettes, but as a monument to her motherhood. Having once learned the relief of contracting her stomach muscles, she could do it now at will and so, when anxious, edge her way better into the day ahead. She didn't fit her hand into the shoes, as she blacked, marooned and browned them, because her hand was too big. Blue shirt, navy blue jumper and denim for the oldest; pale yellow shirt, dark green jumper and denim for the red-haired, the difficult one; white shirt, rust jumper and denim for her favourite.

They ate breakfast then, the older two trying, out of remarkable sensitivity, not to be too excited, the younger one bungling his way right through his mother's heart. She brushed their hairs, hairs that had given her varying degrees of heartburn, and let them fall whatever way they wanted. Black eiderdown, red razors and brown feathery curls. She was a great one for love. She wished he would come soon so she could stop her hands from conjuring over them.

He did. She answered the door to tidiness. Of course, she didn't look at him, but from the corner of her eye she could see ten years of her life and she could smell clean living. He chatted this particular morning because he must have forgotten who she was. She took the children to the cleanest car she would ever see and filed them into the back seat. He checked the front lamp. Her body leaned into his property. She settled them all comfortably, all of them, even the older one, quiet, looking at her, delighted that she was also doing this. She was nearly overcome by clean car smell, the soft music from perfect speakers, not a wire out of place, the dust-free comfort, as in the cars of rich people, or young men excited with their purchase. She moved their clothes, moved them, rearranged, so she could smell this for longer. She could go away on a date in a car like this. Jesus, Chrissie, where are your morals? Just for comfort.

She pulled her body and life out of his success, waved goodbye and said, 'Well, now you're free Chrissie. Do. Do.' She had not relearned yet that people were allowed minutes or days to make plans. She stepped inside. The house was a space enclosed of function with nothing to function about. A craziness came into her soul and she went to the boat to peep-tom on her own children and their father parking the car and leaving the island.

She did not look like a woman who was hiding and she placed herself in the waiting room for the perfect view of the people and the matters which were her concern. A man and his children passed before her. The man was not talking to the children because he was organising tickets, safety and time. The children tottered behind him, plodding aimlessly on to the boat, not sure of what navigation meant. Those were her children.

Excuse me, sir – those children there. They grew to outrageous sizes in my womb and split me open in order to get out. In time my body healed a little. Now they break my heart but it's my cunt that cries. That man with them was my husband. He was – I suppose, still is – English and a class up from me on top of that. We went on our honeymoon to see his parents. Can you imagine that for a honeymoon? Mind you, I was dying to see his parents because of the romance. He hadn't told them he was getting married, so I was welcomed first as a nice Irish friend, then I went outside to the apple blossom while he told them the news. It had nothing to do with me. They and he then brought me in and gave me tea, welcoming me, I suppose as a wife (which I hated), his mother shocked but, still, she gave me sympathetic looks. The sleeping arrangements were changed with the heavy-footedness that should be reserved only for funerals. It was a cruel thing to do to her but I went along with it because I was dazzled by him and hadn't grown up. How desperate, how terrible, sir, that there is not even a nod of friendship left after all that dazzlement.

One of the passing men looked at her – he could have sworn that she was talking to herself. She wore a black coat and a golden scarf. Her eyes pierced holes in her heart. That time, her parents-in-law – the first time the law had any bearing on her life – took a photo of them, her and their son. She couldn't remember which of the parents had held the camera. She had worn a machine-knit cardigan that reached to her knees and had a four-inch waistband. The sister of a woman at work had knit it along with hundreds of others and had made a fortune. She then got a brain tumour and died. These facts were there, immovable from memory. Facts were such harsh things. They could not be changed. Not even the frills of them could be turned about to make it easier. His mother had fussed a little but then got to like her. Chrissie, rather strange name. His young sister had said that she had two chins. It was a good honeymoon, she thought, although she had nothing to compare it with.

They had come back and moved into a house that he had found. Her heart was nearly crushed by the symmetry of the street. It took her months to know which house was hers. She talked about this as if it was, what indeed it was, the greatest crime committed against her to date. But it was only a beginning. In no time at all she was a dormitory sleeper giving out breast milk and sex. The men ran out of the houses into the morning, into cars, and zoomed away to life, glad to be out of that mêlée for a while. She wore a dressing gown late and tried to sleep her life away with the babies. Sometimes he said, 'You can have the car, I'm getting a lift today', or 'You can have the car, I don't need it today', and she let it sit there in the garage because she had nowhere to go – she was with babies. On those days she sometimes fidgeted with the car keys absently.

There he was now, on the way up the gangplank. There they were, her babies, being led away like lambs to people they didn't know, because of the law. That red hair was her brother's.

When she said she was leaving 'this good house' to go live in a dump, he said, 'Not with my children, you're not.'

'Yes I am,' she said. 'And they're my children.'

She had a point. Then he said that none of the children were his. This was a man's privilege – they are, they aren't, they are, they aren't. So she said, 'Yes, they are all your children.'

These days he kept telling each of them how like himself they were. Panic, she presumed. They were gone into the stomach of the boat and she could do nothing now but be free.

This holiday, he intended to wipe her out for a week. His

parents would not mention her and gradually the children would stop talking of her because they would learn that they got no response. He would bring them to clean places; his father's car would be spotless and Chrissie's favourite would long for the hole in his uncle's car that his mother sometimes borrowed, through which he could see the road. Chrissie's favourite would also think that they didn't even want him to talk about her, but what else was there to talk about? He would become quiet. Chrissie's husband had ideas about how to get rid of Chrissie out of her children's heads – all of these ideas taking as their central point, money, tidiness and other states related to tidiness. Surely if he showed them the proper way to live, they would forget about her with her unabashed poverty, her steeliness in the face of what they would not have had to suffer if she'd behaved herself. But would they forget her dreams? He would try. This holiday he would succeed.

Chrissie heard him thinking hate down the gangplank, through the waiting room, into her bones. Still, she could hardly complain. In her bitterer days she had passed through a town where he'd brought them once. They had previously told her about it with rushed excitement. Now she was going through this town on a train, unexpectedly. The name jumped at her, tearing ribbons in her stomach. She frantically talked to all three of them at the same time, gorging them into her, so that they wouldn't become distracted by him. On the way back, going through the town again, she relented and they smiled at her, one single long smile, for remembering. She had looked out the window far away, far away, letting her eyes fill up again, the name of the town giving her a headache.

She walked away from the pier. The woman in the black coat and the golden scarf with her hands in her pockets fidgeting for the need of something between them, a blanket, a pan or a child.

Sir, if only I hadn't had them. Can you imagine how I would look, how I would be? If you can, you've a better imagination than me. And maybe it's not imagination you've got, because, after all, I do remember not having them – do remember me. You don't even know me now nor then. Still, they're not really children, they're my children. Indeed you're right, sir, they would have had, could have had, a different life if I had not been foolish. But who are you to say that I am a saleable life to be traded against what you call a normal home? My next-door neighbour's son – eighteen – was a vegetarian. His father, one Sunday, cornered him and tried to force meat down his throat. I heard the screams but thought that they could not possibly be coming from our street. It changed my mind about normality.

Another man could have sworn that the woman said something to him.

No, sir, I'm afraid I didn't speak to you.

She swung past him, her face showing a brilliant contempt.

Contempt like this is living art, sir. If only I hadn't had them, I could go now, and be gone when he came back and never have to see him again, which is, after all, what the whole thing was about. My babies. My poor dear babies. How could I think them out of existence? Once though, I bumped into my husband on the street. We both nearly stopped, forgetting for a split second the last seven years, not remembering for a tiny flash that we hated each other. We said hello because it was too late not to, then we sprang as if burned, up the street in opposite directions, which is the way we should always have been going. I thought sorrow, vengeance, then pity-for-me who couldn't go, stuck on an island full of Catholics because of a husband. Sir.

When Chrissie got home she noticed the dead crocuses. They lay flat in the window boxes like purple, yellow and white snails' slime and they drew her down with them, even though their obviousness should have been dismissible.

Because such darkness does not have survivors to tell tales, Chrissie woke next morning, Sunday, with a new approach floating in her dreams. She went walking in the park, wearing a red jacket, a silver scarf, and carelessly twiddled a daffodil. But the park was full of men with children. Men who ten years previously would have been in pubs at this time, drinking their Sunday morning pint before going home to dinner and the wife. Now they were embarrassedly running round after the children, putting them awkwardly on swings, exercising their rights. She had never been that fond of parks, but today this one was particularly bad, even worse than normal – it had become the exchange point. Mostly mischievous children, who knew when big people had had it up to here, and some serious, hardened children were passed from one sullen parent to another. In that brief moment, the parents, big children one and all, tried to hold on to dignity, self-righteousness and con-tempt – poor excuses for what was once love. The mischievous children took advantage of the moment, before being whipped into line by the receiving parent, who didn't wish to appear out of control. Chrissie sidled out of the park as if it had nothing to do with her and she was just a normal Sunday-morning woman thinking about lust.

At the bus stop a child had well and truly got the better of her father – she was eight, he was forty:

'I'm going to tell Mammy.'

'Fucking tell your mammy whatever you like. You just do that.'

You'd think he was talking to a six-footer.

'Yes. Just do that.' He caught his chest. 'She has me heart broke. Her effin' mother, excuse the language, has her ruined.'

Chrissie's approach for positivity was getting buffeted on

the outside, so she headed for home again.

Why couldn't she have put up with it – what was so difficult about One House, One Man? She'd done everything else for him, sat on a chair one night, feeling an intrauterine device sear through her insides up to her tonsils. It was only supposed to be for the lower, the dangerous, regions, but it left its pains in every other part of her body too. The doctor had talked about politics as she embedded the foreign object in her pink womb. That helped Chrissie not to think of the mutilation and the pain.

When she had met him first she had gone to bed a lot between letters, taking their love with her and hiding it under the blankets, even wrapping it inside her so no one could steal it from her. How more faithful could she have been? She had rung his telephone number even when she knew he wasn't there just to hear it ring. Hadn't she had children for him? For him. Certainly, it could not have been for herself. How much more could she have done? In the first year when they fought she said she was sorry, always sorry, and meant it. Later when they fought, she put her arms tight around the baby and made an outsider of him. It was her only possible defence against the words of a healthy man. They walked home one time. She pleaded for a taxi as her monthly blood seeped from her insides. He, with the money in his pocket, refused. He thought that she would forget that. Chrissie found it hard to remember now the love that must have been there. Every time the word came unbidden she flicked her eyes as if she were a train timeboard. Move on. She had written a message for him once on a dusty bus, that much she did allow herself to think upon: 'If you pass here, you'll have walked the same steps as me. Love, Chrissie.'

When he had got the divorce papers she was raging that she hadn't thought of it first or even had had one procured by using a friend's London address, and she could have said, You moron, I did that years ago. He would have got the papers in a serious fashion, in his own country; she could just see him, as if cutting out something distasteful. She would have done it in style and gone for wine afterwards.

Her children. Where are they now? Liking the sea, she hoped. Not afraid, she hoped. Last week the middle one had said, 'We have this couch in our father's. You can make a bed out of it.'

'Do you indeed, and is it black leather and does it have a silver spring and is the shape of a pregnant woman's body branded on it?'

'What did you say, Mammy?'

'Nothing.'

'And we have this tape.'

'Really! And is there a song on it called "Make Me an Island"? Ha!'

'How did you know that?'

She slammed the door: my couch! And the next door: my tape! By Jesus, wait until your twenty-first. See that corner, I'm going to get you into it and tell you about your precious father. I wouldn't want to do it for a while, ten or fifteen years or so, because I'd be afraid of deranging you or giving you a complex. What I do to save your mental health! But it will keep. This corner here. And you'll know then from where I get this tight lip that gets tighter by the month. This corner. That is, if we're still in this flat, of course. And if it matters then.

On Sundays before and after the first was born, but not after the second, they used to go visiting. Sunday morning loveliness first, reminiscent in its own way of polished shoes and purity. Sex somewhere between twelve and two. Dinner before or after. Never as good as mother's. Not even once. Then fear would descend upon her. The weekend was over now – Sunday afternoon could not offer any opium, any panacea. Monday isolation loomed and she wouldn't see anyone for another week. So she would inveigle him to go visiting on the pretext that a drive would be good after their lovemaking. He would have wanted to sleep. First year, they would head either for C and R's or P and K's – next year, they headed more often for P and K's because P had a baby too. Third year, equal again because R had a child now. C and R were different from P and K in smallish ways, not in any major way that one expects from our belief that the individual is unique. (Not to mention the set of two individuals.) C and R bought a dearer suite of furniture but P and K spent what they had saved by buying the plastic suite on a superior three-in-one hi-fi set. Both C and R and P and K bought dining-room suites, washing machines and do-it-themselves combinations on/in which to store their wedding presents. Chrissie would sit dazed. She never knew the difference between makes of food-mixers and was deficient in her appreciation of woods. Should they have stayed at home? Perhaps if they had, C and R or P and K might have visited them in the way that frightened young married couples will drop in on each other to check that things have not gone too far wrong. At least in her own home she could have had some control over the conversation.

'When is the baby due, Chrissie?'

'What baby?' She felt her womb and pretended she'd thought it was someone else they were asking about. 'Sorry, me? Oh me, eh, four months.'

Whose house was she in? Was it C and R's or P and K's? They would then drive home, or rather her husband would drive home and she would look out the window at Sunday visitors who had been out looking for people like themselves, some of them successful, some of them unsuccessful, missing-passing the people they were looking for on both journeys, as they – the people they were looking for – looked for them and missed-passed them. She hadn't seen C and R or P and K since. Wonder what they were like now? Would she have even one word to say to them? Probably one hundred and sixteen Sunday afternoons. Each.

Her children would be there by now.

'Daddy's taking us to Ingaland. Why do you never take us there, Mammy?'

There were three possible answers to that and then the real one. She opted for silence.

Once they had gone to a hotel to meet some manager or other from her husband's job. She sat on the soft seat, looking at the glass doors, at cars, and porters, at excitement, at sex, at beauty. Her husband ranted and railed about privilege, about class. Who was he to talk? She knew nothing about these things, only about freedom. The manager joined them, and she still looked out the glass doors. Lights, car lights, were coming on, cheating the summer night. The excitement was getting hotter.

'What did you say, Chrissie?'

'Sorry, nothing. Excuse me I must go to . . .'

Jesus, the toilets were fit for living in. Freshen your mouth right now. Twenty p for a pre-pasted toothbrush. Imagine! She hoped she had two tens. She did.

How could she remember it, that brush? It was blue plastic with a screw-on top, a plastic brush, a smell of fresh toothpaste. It was travel, travel bags, trains, talking to strangers, new cities, flat hot countries, mirages. She put it in her bag for when she would need it. It was that, and that sort of thing, which made her leave 'this good house', 'the good house', 'your home'. She forgot for a moment in the saying of it that she had three children and by then it was too late. Still, they were the only mistake she hadn't made. Her time would come.

'You're forcing me to consider hitting you.' That was worse, only in some senses, than being hit. She waited to be hit. She never was, just starved. But her time would come some day for revenge.

By the day of the actual split she was so tired that all she thought of was sleep. The split itself wasn't such a big thing to her at all. As things deteriorated to a noticeable level, relatives started calling on her, during the day, anything to stop the whole thing from falling apart. Anything. At least she wasn't on her own any more. Maybe if they'd done it sooner? She wished she had the nerve to ask them to let her go to bed for a short sleep, just a little sleep, instead of talking to her. Now that they were here, could they mind the children for an hour? Immediately they'd come in the door, she'd think of her bed. Remember that Sunday they'd joined the queue for parking cars outside the church, like any other suburban couple, with the country mother in the front seat beside the man, the driver, the daughter or daughter-in-law in the back? When the rumpus erupted because they'd missed mass – the times had been changed six months before – Chrissie was fast asleep. The sun streamed in on her and, despite the annoyance, they let her sleep on, her mother nearly sympathetic.

She decided to clean the kitchen – always better than remembering, and it came naturally to her now, but she knew that it was daft to do housework when she wasn't confined. Yet what could she do? In the end she used the long weekend to feel sorry for herself sometimes, with good reason (it was also therapeutic and it saved her from feeling inadequate), and the rest of the time to become a new Chrissie yet again. She talked to herself, went for walks dressed in white, black, purple, told secrets to the one tree in the avenue, and kicked expensive cars on her way home at night. By the time they came back, half of her wanted to squeeze radiance into their faces, another half would have passed them in the street and pretended it had run away from home. But her favourite smiled first and that settled that.

FURTHERMORE, SUSAN

Susan, great to see you, God it's been far too long, and you look great too. No, I'm not telling lies, I'm just trawling for you to say the same to me. Oh, I'm fine, fine, a little washed out, a shade disappointed with life, but just a shade, that's not too bad. I'm a Scorpio, though, and the main thing about them is that they always cope; yes, I know that the main thing about them is supposed to be that they're creative, but that's only when they're not up to their necks coping. The business of keeping house could get to you though, couldn't it? All that changing of bin bags – still, never mind, here we are. I'll have a gin and tonic – yeah, it's come to that. God, little did we know that those bastard publicans who wouldn't serve us pints were actually doing us a favour. Ah, those were the days, when I was fascinated by the workings of the body, only the interesting bits of course, they seemed to be leading some-where. It would have suited me a lot better to have been a bit more fascinated by what was happening to my kidneys. I see they've ruined this pub too, there's so much old pine in pubs now, you'd think half time you were in a coffin. And there's your mate, the crawler, the one who goes arse-travelling up to people's tonsils, all you ever see of him is the soles of his shoes out someone's hole... Sorry, sorry, I keep forgetting that you're so sensitive and well bred. So, tell us all. How's the new job; any nice men? Sorry, I don't mean to trivialise your measured march upwards, great to see someone still hawkling up the ladder. I don't know how you bear it, I wouldn't be able for all that prancing about. In Údarás na Gaeltachta? Really! Great all the Irish names everywhere now, I suppose it must mean something, us and the Jews concentrating on speaking our old tongues. I believe they've got further. The young fellow upstairs has just got a job as a doorkeeper in the morgue in Vincent's Hospital. You're right, funny thing to come into my mind, after language. Anyway, fancy that for a job. His black suit is sort of shiny, like a nineteen fifties priest's. He comes home in the evening all solemn, having forgotten how to talk to people who haven't been recently bereaved. All that hushed deference trying to break out into an ordinary tone of voice! Some evenings I think he's going to choke. I suppose he'll be well practised when it comes to his own turn. Or else he'll be like the midwives who have a baby themselves – by God, that soon changes the way they see the woman in the bed! Did I ever tell you that I want to be buried in the nude. Another drink? Some smart-arse told me that you can't drown your sorrows because they can swim, but I suppose a gin might soak their toes. Well tell us about the holiday. Really! Really! Imagine that! Well you can't argue with an allegory. I waken up every morning saying that. Since sixteen hundred, eight hundred and seventy-nine shipwrecks have been confirmed off the Wexford coast, did you not know that? No, I suppose not, it's a fairly useless fact really, isn't it? Mind you, it's no more useless than a lot of others I have up my sleeve. You want to hear the songs, they go on for a fortnight. I was thinking about shipwrecks the other day. You know that thing about women and children first, I don't think it applies any more. Not if you look at the lists of the dead and survived. You see that picture there, you think it's just a woman, well it's not, she's a *Titanic* survivor – makes her look different, doesn't it? Now that you know. Yeah, me too, I used to think that she was just a woman. Look at those two girls under the picture, they keep moving about from seat to seat, hoping to make the right decision. About what? you'd wonder. I went to northern Spain that nobody calls Spain any more – they're too intent on distancing themselves from their past and trying to slip into a future unnoticed – the land of the clothes peg, pegged on every open package on every person's shelf to keep goods fresh, even on the sheet music of the orchestra to keep it from blowing away. The concert was great. For dinner there was a lot of Jacques Cousteau on a plate. When I came back from my holiday-making there were new houses on the street, very unsettling. But then I don't walk on the tarred bits in parks, I walk on the grass, part of my history. Dublin's changing – my neighbour says that mournfully at least once a week, but you can tell that she's secretly curious, you'd never know what they will change it into. The whole world's changing, Martha, I say, bad, as if I was fucking ninety-five, sorry about the language, I do keep forgetting that some words make you take cover, like an American. Of course, I mean a certain kind of American, I know it's a big country. Even my Dublin has changed and I'm not here a wet week. My first flat is no longer a flat, it's bloody Locke's restaurant. The starters are worth two months of what my rent used to be. I sat at a table in it one night, oh yes, it's not only you that has come a long way. I got to eat in my bedroom. I spent the time staring at people because they were picking at twenty pound starters in places where things of great import had happened to me. You know the way you're supposed to have a loyalty to the first? Well, I was trying to remember, because I knew it had happened under the leg of my chair. I couldn't concentrate on the dinner, I missed all those dear tastes. Do you know what he does now? He massages ley lines in Derry, maybe that's why the loyalty had difficulty in seriously materialising. Locke's, there were Lockes at our primary school; we gave them dog's abuse, because someone has to be given it. I worried at times about it, but I liked belonging to the majority then. Now I know that the anarchists paint better slogans, art almost. I wonder are all the Lockes jittery now because of our bullying? One of them came to the secondary with me, she became weird, her conversations became ambushes. She had a nervous breakdown and left. It was the day we were doing 'Among Schoolchildren'. W.B. Yeats. They put that poem on the course because it has the word 'school' in it, even the teachers don't know what it's about. Having a breakdown may have been wise. So there we are, that's all the news I have. Why didn't I tell you about Simon? Ah, it was a mess really, I thought I'd better not talk about it until I'd forgotten it. It was a bit disappointing, I was disappointed in myself. My Uncle Joseph had some interesting things to say about it. No he's not dead, he may not be alive but he's definitely not dead. He tore Simon to bits, subtle as a train wreck, and me still going about with the taste of him in my mouth. How the hell would I know what happened? It's hard being a sailor's girl, I suppose. I remember when I was small hearing about a woman who was going to marry a sailor, a ship's engineer they said, which on further enquiry I discovered to be the same as a sailor. They clucked and clucked about her being on her own a lot, and I remember thinking, well she was on her own before she met him, so can't she just keep on going the same way? But now I know they were right; being married to a sailor is a different kind of being on your own. Well, I know I wasn't married to him, just nearly. You can tell how people would make love by the way they smoke their cigarettes. Simon varied a lot, big deep drags, gentle puffs under the table in recognition of the rights of you non-smoking, non-swearing people. Susan, for God's sake don't look so serious, ribbing is a form of envy. I couldn't do without my bad language because I'm not as good a person as you and if you believe that... But, as I was saying, Simon always finished his cigarette, even if he was uncomfortable. He'd look at the butt carefully when he was stubbing it out. He was kind — if he ever had to laugh at someone he knew, tears would come to his eyes. Must have bawled about me out on the ocean. No, I'm not being too hard on myself, just removing the sting. Naw, we weren't suited, he made me uncomfortable; I would clear all the books and tapes away before he came so he wouldn't see the crap I was pouring into my brain. At least I always had time, ships do dock in the night and rarely before they're due. I followed two people in the supermarket yesterday, listening to them fighting the piece out. Susan, of course I did it surreptitiously, and if I had been caught - so! they couldn't prove anything. As a result of tailing this row, I forgot to buy the Weetabix. The things people say to each other! But at least those two have the rest of the month to let things settle. They have the morass of family chitchat, you can bury a lot under that — it's pointless asking a man to take out the rubbish if he's on the Gulf of Mexico. But he wasn't as smart as he thought he was; he showed me a picture of himself as a baby and then I saw it in my local all-night shop, it was just a postcard. And I came across a poem he had written to me, it bore a striking resemblance to something else that I had just seen in a book. Not like me to be reading poetry anthologies and I suppose he had banked on that. It was a terrible blow. When I sort of wrangled the conversation near to the matter, not straight out, of course not, he copped that I had copped, and said it was just a joke. Some laugh. Made me feel like a no one, not the best thing to be walking about on a wet day.

If there was just me, in the flat he keeps, he never set the table, the way he did for his proper friends, just threw the things on it; you'd think it was the men from the threshing that were in. He made me remember my past in wicked flashes and there's no getting over those. In the end, having sex with each other would have required a certain humility on both our parts and neither of us had the training for that. I suppose you think that sailors have their own national way of letting women down. Not really. The end was identical to every other finale I've ever had. Except I don't have to worry too much about bumping into him. On the last night he said that he was having trouble with his hernia but I told him he couldn't have a hernia because he was all brain. There's your woman who was in that big film, they only put her in it because her father's so rich they knew people would go to see how bad she could be. That's Ireland for you. And there's the Monaghan goalie – I know, Susan, that it's a woman, but did you not know that Monaghan and Laois Ladies were in Croke Park last October. Yes, Ladies. And there's an unusually high number of women being pointlessly called that here tonight. No, it's the goalie all right. I skivvied for her parents for a while, for pocket money, when I was at school. When she grew up, even though she wasn't one herself, she married a Catholic and had a baby on the honeymoon. Fast movers them Catholics. Ah, football. Did you see the Rangers supporters on the telly last night, dancing away, swinging from their hips. Makes you want to marry a Protestant, or maybe it's a Scotsman I mean. Yeah, I suppose you're right, you usually are. I've been thinking, all the ex-boyfriends of mine that I still see have line-free faces but every morning is dug into mine like a trench. Do you know what I found myself doing yesterday? Washing the Scrabble pieces. From now on there'll be no more of that. I'm going to lighten up, carry a playroom around with me in my heart. Your party? Of course I'll go, but don't introduce me to any nice men, I think I'm about to get one myself and I don't want to be tempted. Is that your coat? Lovely cut to it.

BEATRICE

Maybe it was the day that had caused it. A warm, over-generous June day, fifteen hours. The sky had been full of sun. The sort of day you are afraid to commit to memory in case it cracks if you stare. Beatrice Sherry had spent it being unbearably happy for no reason at all. Well, that is if you think fresh air so tasty it can be swallowed and such sun, such sun, no reason at all.

All these days now, she thought about what it might have been that caused it and how it happened. It was easier that way, blaming or thanking some vague *it*. Surely no one would expect her to say that she had done it herself, had landed herself here. Ah, but she had. She had stood beside him deliberately at the end of the party; they had been introduced casually as happens at aimless holiday parties flung together at the end of holiday nights in the west of Ireland. She found herself beside him, oh yes, found herself, then a waltz came on, I don't waltz, he said, I'll teach you, she said, and when she moved closer to get into the dance position a warm shiver like a needle went up between her legs and whistled to her head, making her feel faint. There was blood everywhere carousing, carousing through her veins. She didn't teach him to waltz, and next thing they found themselves at the door, ah yes, found themselves, he supposedly going – it would be easier to test the thing now – she supposedly staying. She held the door open for him, as if it was her house, which it wasn't; they each moved about one-eighth of one inch closer to the other, just enough to ensure that they could not then draw back. And no one knew whose tongue was drinking whose. They found themselves in his place (at least, he had a key) and they stripped each other slowly, rubbing their bare skin together, their tongues resting inside each other's mouths, or sucking ferociously, or gently licking. Her breasts felt sharp and brazen against him, she lowered her mouth and kissed and gently pulled his nipples. They hardened so readily he was shocked. They touched as much as they could stand, held each other's faces in their hands, and then pulled the breath from each other in one ecstatic coming that left them near tears and bewildered. They couldn't bear to take their arms from around their bodies.

But morning had to come. They slipped away – he to work, she to more holiday – afraid to say a word. She was terrified.

(It's not that she minded having an affair – she never liked that word, it was more like cold curry than what it was supposed to be – no one minds having an affair. Mind you, the one she'd had five years ago was just that, cold curry. I suppose you'd call it an affair; she met him twice, the time she met him and once more. The time she met him she was a bit drunk and she thought that he was the loveliest looking man since . . . since . . . God forgive her, she had it off with him in the car, well, there was nowhere else to go, and anyway, she'd never done that before, even though she was nearly thirty-one. Maybe most people never did? They even went to the trouble of taking all their clothes off, except for their socks. That trouble, that attention to the detail of each other's bodies, convinced her the next day that he was worth meeting again. It never struck her, or she forgot, that it was she who had insisted on all their clothes coming off. She also forgot how he kissed, which she thought was a bad sign, but still, you can't remember everything.

Between that night and the second time, a number of things were done. First there was the phone call, a few letters, and then the countdown. She had written him a letter telling him that she could meet him. Just to be sure of his flight – she didn't want to arrive at the wrong time and waste an hour or, more important, spend an hour looking so conspicuous that someone would be bound to notice her. A friend of hers was caught at the airport once; mind you, the woman who caught her was on her way back from a secret abortion in London so she could hardly talk – still, she enclosed an envelope addressed by herself to herself.

Although his other letters and postcards had always got through between the gas bills and the flat circulars, it would be foolish to risk getting caught at this late stage, hence the self-addressed envelope. Noticed by whom? Caught by whom? A husband of course. It wouldn't have been an affair without a husband. Yes, she had a husband, not a very good one, not a very exciting one, but a husband. (She was younger then and less cautious about husbands.)

She had read the letters again before writing the arrangements to him. They had varied; she looked for signs of intelligence in them. Once he had used the word 'generic' in an odd way and she had had to look it up in the dictionary – she wasn't quite sure if you could use it that way. You could, that was a good sign. In other letters he wrote about boring things, work and the like – he couldn't seriously believe that she was interested in the engineering possibilities of bridges over the M1, but she supposed he wanted to fill up the page until he could get down to the real part of the letter, it was only decent to do that. The real parts of his letters always began with 'Well

Beatrice'. Then he would reminisce about how they had met. She just had to read the 'Well Beatrice' bit and she'd lose her head altogether. She'd remember how they looked into each other's eyes as they came together in the car, which was hard to do and also brave of them really because you'd never know what you'd see in someone's eyes at a time like that. And then she'd remember the texture of his skin which was extraordinary, silky, like a precious memory from somewhere. Anyway, no need to go over all that again, he was on his way here for the weekend. She had felt a little obscene including the SAE without the stamp, an Irish stamp would be no good in England – an AE I suppose you'd call it. It was very premeditated: you couldn't explain it away by saying, I don't know what came over me. After his reply the countdown began.

DAY 5   Woke having had very bad dreams. Neck of nightdress soaking wet. Oh God, am I coming down with flu? By ten o'clock was all right so knew it was just guilt. The dream had been awful though. By twelve was normal again.

DAY 4   Had a terrible row with husband which I let get out of hand probably so I could say, see! he deserves me to go and have an affair.

DAY 3   Went into a panic about what I will do about car. It would be better to hire one so no one could recognise the number. Is licence in date?

DAY 2   Husband announces he is going away. With car. God I love him he's so good. I now have peace to book a hotel and hire a car.

DAY 1   Came out of car-hire place puce in the face...You'd think I wanted it for I don't know what, a bank robbery or worse.

She met him, by now mortified, really, and doubtful that this was going to be worth the trouble. There were real people at the airport waiting for genuine reasons. There was a father hugging his son, his face trembling, and his daughter-in-law. Ah, his daughter-in-law, he squeezed her to him and let his face collapse. She had taken his lovely son but he couldn't blame her for that. How he loved that daughter-in-law. But no, they wouldn't stay at home. His wife was dead.

Beatrice recognised the engineer and immediately thought, I need a drink. They had a pint of Guinness and three cigarettes each. She hadn't been able to eat earlier, so this was her breakfast. She drove to the hotel half drunk, amused at herself by now. At the first red light she leaned over and ran her lips over his face. Might as well. He kissed back and then she remembered. Surely things would be all right. Surely they would be worth it. But she had forgotten again how he kissed by the time they reached the hotel.

They had sex and he fell asleep – honest to God. Actually it was only passable, she had much better at home, she decided. If he had stayed awake, she mightn't have had time to think that. His skin wasn't soft at all. She listened to a woman next door torturing her child: 'Why do you make my life such a misery? I might stop being your mother, I might just do that, or you might give me a heart attack and what would you do then? With no mother.' Really she should get up and ring the ISPCC. Wimbledon was vaguely on the television. But she fell asleep too.

Later they went for a walk. And that was when the real trouble started. The man said some pointless thing. He was not adventurous with his words. She liked words, things to remember. Maybe if she gave him a pen and paper and asked him to write a letter? It would at least pass some of the time. One hour had gone by and he'd only said a thing or two, both of them about engineering. Jesus, please, I'll learn to pray again

if you give this man a few words to say. You think three hours
is a short time? Well, if you're doing nothing and saying nothing, it's one hundred and eight thousand seconds, or so it
seems. She made some terrible excuse and escaped to her own
home.

That had been the death of some small emotional insurance.
Beatrice left his letters where they were for a few months because she was afraid to find out that she should have known.
One night she took them out and skimmed over them
quickly. They were sometimes like school essays, 'Christmas
is a busy time', but then they could be surprising with the sure-
ness of an entitled life lived. As she burned them she tried to
feel something, but nothing would come. He couldn't have
been that bad. There's that postcard, the blue water hissing
now in the flames and the word 'generic' in the odd place,
gone for ever. So really, she'd never actually had an affair.)

And now she was terrified, because nothing could ever be
the same again, nothing, day nor night nor season, nor logic
nor sense. The day was Thursday. She went back to her design
job four days later. They had met once again. On Friday his
wife had joined him. It hadn't, after all, been his place, he had
the key to his friend's flat for when he was working in these
parts. Even this became an intimate revelation. Because it was
the weekend, and such a beautiful one, his nurse wife was join-
ing him to spend it by the sea. What sea? Beatrice had forgotten the Atlantic behind her. Her husband, R, joined her also
and as far as she could remember, they talked normally.

On Saturday at a quarter past five Beatrice managed a quick
hour in the pub. From the newsagent's she had spotted Him at
the door, pecking his wife goodbye, she who was obviously
on the way to the beach. Beatrice told her husband, with unmannerly haste, that she was going to head off alone for a
walk. She wouldn't be long. He said OK. Beatrice followed

Him into the pub. 'Oh goody,' he said. 'I like furtive women.' They did not strip each other in the pub because you have to be careful about these things. She stayed one hour and left quickly when she saw her, by now perplexed, husband walking past the window.

JUNE THE NEXT YEAR

I packed and met my friend in the Pembroke for lunch. She knows, so she gave me this diary as a joke so I can record the best and the worst, as if I would. I have ten days, in the middle of which R will join me for the weekend. R, my husband, don't, don't hassle me. The train went through the usual places, which should be settling, but train journeys always fill me up. Will this throw my whole life into a sickening chaos? I have to hope that it won't; I have to hope that it will. That's why it would be better not to find out. Will we be able to speak to each other, will we be able to talk to each other? But first of all, will I be able to speak at all and will I give it away by not being able to do anything but stammer and swallow? Or should I say, will he like me as much as I like him? I am doing this because ... I wish the train journey was over. I have one definite arrangement but the rest may be torture for me. I may become a sixteen-year-old unwoman waiting to be wanted. Ah no! He is not cruel. Hopefully. I don't have to mean 'hopefully'. I don't believe that men you sleep with once then become cruel. Why, why am I thinking this nonsense then? I spend the rest of the journey seeing him seeing me.

My B&B is quite all right. Passed the day being nervous and wishing I had half a dozen children to occupy me. I am to meet him at six o'clock. That will give us time. I wish it was five to six. It's only four. I went to the pub at three minutes to six and he wasn't there of course, so I went to the toilet and spoke out loud to myself as if I was talking to him. If you do that to me I will die. Honestly I will. I knew that I should have been saying, if you do that to me I will kill you, but that's not what came out. Went down again. Sat at bar, with my back to the door, in a delighted nervous mess. He came in and I couldn't look, my eyes burned so much. My face took on a life of its own. I smiled, then I looked. He thought I looked lovely and he meant that it was great to see me and I knew why I was there. He didn't touch me and I thought I would split open for the want of his skin. Then it dawned on me that he thought it was his prerogative to touch me first. We talked through an hour – he has had it with marriage, houses, monogamy. Up to his neck, he says. Up to those beautiful balls of yours, I would have thought, if I hadn't been too polite. I was less worried by marriage than he, less immersed in its pointlessness. As he got gloomier I realised that I thought of mine as the state of having or being an identical twin. I suppose that meant mine wasn't working. We were thinking, too, like people who were not with each other, so we had brandy. I got down from my stool to pay for it, which was not necessary, and made sure that I touched his leg accidentally as I sat back up. That released us from a dreadful wondering, wondering whether the lives we'd just described could possibly be ours and if so how had we let them happen. One touch and we were free. We couldn't wait to finish the brandy. The man beside me didn't want his wife to hang up her coat, fur, on the back of the door. Anyone could lift it, he said. She was needled. She was out for a drink, she reminded him, and couldn't give a fuck about the coat.

They went to 'his' place. He said he had the key and stayed there when he was working around here. His friend who owned it was away a lot, mostly in Belfast doing a course in peace studies in . . .

'Yes, you told me,' she said intimately.

He looked surprised, wary almost. He couldn't remember telling her.

'Last year.'

'Oh yes.'

She didn't have an orgasm, which was very unlike her, she could usually have one just thinking. A blessing perhaps, or maybe not. She tried to get him to help her, which was new to her. He was reluctant. He got up from the bed quickly and said, 'You women are always so superior, holding back.'

She could have said one of many things. Touchy, aren't we? might have sufficed as the kindest one of them. What she said was, 'Just you wait until the next time.' That relaxed him. He wanted to go back to the pub, so they went.

Morning came as if it and they had been together for ever. But he left, mid-sentence, to go to work, leaving the oddest non-arrangement hanging between them. She could ring him up at half four and then he'd see how he was fixed.

I went to the newsagent's, bought a book and waited in the B&B. And waited some more. I read, pausing now and then as the tips of my nipples sent a glandular earthquake rolling down inside me. So inside me. I have just eaten and it is now four o'clock. I can ring him soon. Can. Am allowed to. Dear me, what a long way down. I tell myself that I am not nervous, that instead I have a quiet glow. Not an ecstatic one, a quiet one. This glow makes my life easier, seem easier. I'm thinking about my real life at the moment and, because this glow is part of it, it's not so bad. But I'm not confident that he will want to see me tonight. The lack of confidence on my part is not without cause, he doesn't exactly throw the compliments around. He prefers, 'Just like all the women I know', to 'Do you?' or 'Yes?' or 'Really?'. But then he looked so sorry when I said that R was going to join me, genuinely sorry, I blushed it was so obvious. And he rang his friend to let him know that 'we' were there, not just him. He didn't have to do that, it was definitely showing off. Would it be better if it were after half four? But uncertainty has its own enjoyment. I can feel a wetness inside me and I suddenly have to tighten myself, as if I had eaten freezing ice cream.

'I'll be finished here at half five. You could meet me and we could drive up to this other job that I have to check before we decide what to do.' We. 'Fine,' I say, knowing in my heart that I'm too old, good, bright, or something, to be so grateful.

I see the church clock on my way, oh no, oh no, my watch is slow. Will I ever see him again? Ever? Surely he won't have waited, surely he won't, but he had. I would never have had the nerve to be late, I never do, but maybe it was no harm to have kept him waiting, as long as it has turned out all right. Drove to his job, I waited outside, for a minute I imagined that I had been married to him for years. He came out and said, 'Do you want one of the best pints of Guinness in Ireland?' 'Yes,' I said. But I wish to God I knew whether we will go to bed or not. He has the control, this is how he likes it, he's not the sort to like it otherwise. I will have to wait. First, call at the flat. He jumps out of the car, 'Right. Immersion on, water flowers, will be with you in a minute.' Water flowers! That's telling me something, I wish I knew what. 'Now for the Guinness.' He smiles at me, innocently. I'm confused.

Somewhere after too much drink he hints that we might. I'm nearly sober enough to realise that it is a hint and to wish he had said it earlier, but nearly drunk enough to get mad. My passion has been stopped from too much careless yoyoing. We go back, he has a bath, we do. He raises my legs too high, I cannot feel him properly inside like that, I cannot find a touching place for my head. I cannot think this way. I do not care. Am I afraid? I cannot talk to him, he would sniff at my words.

Talk would be too personal for him, he is on top. Then he gave me a scarf that he used to wear to the dole when life was not so good. 'Here,' he said, 'have this.' Yes, rolled off the bed, off me, let's be precise, and handed me a silk scarf that was sitting on the top of his overnight bag. 'Wear it, it will look lovely on you.' He has left me somewhere I'm not used to being. I say something which makes him laugh a lot, I cannot remember what it was, even as he laughs I have forgotten. However, I am glad that I can make him laugh. Eventually I leave and go back to my booked accommodation. He did not ask me to stay, he wants to see me tomorrow. I am glad to get into a bed on my own. Will I try it again? Of course I will.

Beatrice and he spent three evenings together, each one organised at the last minute. That shouldn't have mattered but it did, it piled up undignity.

On the fourth day, R arrived. He and Beatrice went for a drive, after he had consulted the map. They had a drink and she insisted on talking about this man she had met yesterday, she couldn't help it. He says he can't possibly support the Provos any more. That he used to, although he never believed in war. Now he simply can't. R says sarcastically, 'Looks like they've lost a valuable ally, a supporter who didn't believe in war. Must have suffered from a lot of agonised dissonance.' She says, 'Forget it.' He says, 'No, come on, tell me why the man can't, any more.' 'Enniskillen,' she says. 'But that happened ages ago, did the man hear about it late?'

R is alert and watchful. She had better be careful. She gets even drunker and talks about people reaching the edge and about the ferocious pleasure that unacceptable behaviour can bring to a person. She talks too much and gives out bits of information but R doesn't notice or pretends not to. Maybe he's saving it up. Next morning R and Beatrice make an unembarrassed coupling, easy as a kiss. It's what they do sometimes, help themselves to each other. R went back to Dublin at the appointed time, leaving an open sea behind him.

Spent the day checking myself. Why am I doing this? To hear myself described, that's it. In both words and involuntary sounds. I enjoy the agony? Maybe I should take up building houses or something else strenuous, maybe heavy gardening? I remember how the kiss shot needles. I remember the exact sound of his moan when I kissed him first. I want to find new explanations, I don't need words for emotions that I don't know, but for the rest, yes. I want to hear him say confidentially to the barman as he asks, too late, for a carryout, 'Ah, we only see each other twice a year', and to another, 'My wife likes lots of ice'. I want to be in this. I do not see him as in a film. Many times I walk as in a film, watching me, wondering what will happen next, if anything, but when I'm with him it's not watchable, it is. We have no past, will have no future, we will be bigger, brighter than any regrettable thing. But yet it's only my part in it because I have no intention of telling him. He would only think that I was trying to get us involved. I have no perception of him hearing me. My dear.

Beatrice also spent some moments trying not to think of his wife and her own husband. It was easier not to think of R. In the end she took the easy way out and flippantly thought that if they weren't doing the same thing, it wasn't her fault. That would do for now, now being the time before consequences.

I rang him to arrange where we would meet. He mentioned DB's, where we had met before. He said, 'You know where that is?' 'As if I could forget,' I said, with silver in my voice. 'Silly girl,' he said in a downturned tone. Again, I had left myself open for that. I felt like saying, Who the fuck do you think you are? but I didn't. (Later when I told him what I had wanted to say he smiled deliciously. 'I expected that,' he said. Ah! so he is wanting someone open and vulnerable, who will wince, against whom he will appear ever, ever so strong. I was also silly enough to ask if he had ever brought anyone else to this flat. He said, in a high voice, 'I've had the key for eighteen months.' That was just a fleeting something in me, a wish for one little thing from him.)

I turned up at DB's with all my stuff. I had decided to pre-sume now that R had been and gone, that I would stay for the rest of the time with him, or else I had decided to be reckless, I don't know. He twitched when he saw my bag. A man sat with us, a friend of his whom he'd just bumped into. He was waiting for a woman to turn up and it was quite obvious that she wasn't going to. He was downcast. My man didn't look too upbeat about his woman – me – who had. The night was spent, used up, talking to this stood-up man.

We left the pub. He said crossly, 'I'll carry that', taking my bag from me. If I'd insisted that I do it myself, my voice might have wavered, such was the humiliation, embarrassment. I wanted to say, Look, I am . . . whatever, and I don't usually turn up to stay uninvited but I thought that in the circum-stances . . . But when we got outside the pub he crooked his arm and beckoned me to link him. I put my arm in and found myself holding tight. 'Now,' he said, satisfied. I was afraid of such fickleness. He turned the key; I dropped my link because it felt too familiar, let my hand fall into the cold. He turned from the open door and picked it up as if it was his.

He fussed around the settee, the table, making me comfor-table, sensing my unease . . . And then he said, 'First I must ring my wife.' The flat had two large windows, both of them dirty. There was an opening between the bedsitting room and the kitchen, supposedly making separate rooms. I went to the kitchen and tried not to hear but I felt like a keyhole-listener as surely as if I'd had my back bent and my ear pressed. I couldn't see out the window. I raged to myself – talk to your heart's fucking content with some boring stood-up thirty-three-year-old, and as for ringing up your wife, stop trying to impress me. I bet you have the year loaded up with planned weekends, otherwise the two of you would go mad looking at each other. I bet you have ducks flying up your sitting room wall, I bet your bathroom is painted pink or powder blue, I bet you think the alcove at the top of the chipboard built-in cupboard is a feature, in fact that's why the two of you bought the house. I bet you moved out the furry animals from the back window of the car just for me. But worst of all, none of this is my business. Nothing about you is my business.

The extremity of my pathetic gratefulness in the face of his sourness was about to blow up. I simply could not listen any longer, nor could I bear to know that I knew what he would say to me if I tried to explain and that before he had it said I would have forgiven him. In truth, I would have liked to have said goodbye, to put his elbows into my hands and kiss him on the mouth. I wrote a quick 'Sorry I couldn't stay. See you sometime' note. I let myself out quietly and was booked into the nearest B&B before he had got off the phone, I bet. I curled up in bed like an armadillo. All night I heard the sound of seagulls out there being plaintive, scratching the sky as if it was glass. If only it was winter I might be blessed with a quiet body. If the fires were lit in rooms, they might take some of the heat out of me.

Beatrice had to wonder for a while why she had done it. There had been the lush devouring, the agile taste of mouths in the morning, long arched fingers moving slowly in the right places. She knew what it hadn't been; she would not have held him just for the sake of holding him. As well as that, she said in conversation, 'yes indeed' when really she meant 'no'. She had never smiled at him without knowing that she was doing it; she would never have told him the truth. But surely there was no need for him to demolish it so completely. Yet there was, a terrible need.

Beatrice tried to get her imagination to mend the holes in her understanding. She knew he had loved her passion when it opened, as is necessary, but he had also found it unacceptable, too uninnocent. I even guided his hand, she thought. Not only that, she had switched the light back on after he had turned it off. And she had kept her eyes wide open. Wider.

Oh, why not take the blame myself? she thought, days cannot do things of their own accord. It was worth it to remember herself in a straight blue dress, a zip from the top to three-quarters way down, a slit from the bottom to join the zip. Even in the dark she liked new cities.

DAY EVERY DAY

Went away to my town with R. The water in the sea, for that, after all, is all it is, was white with cold.

BIRTH CERTIFICATES

'Call me Regina. There's nothing so daft-sounding as Miss Clarke. Some like Mrs, but Miss is stretching it, I always think,' Miss Clarke, Miss Regina Clarke, said to Maolíosa, shaking her hand heartily.

It's like as if she's shaking hands from her nipple out, thought Maolíosa, at the same moment also thinking, what a ridiculous thing to imagine. What made me think of that?

'Sit down. No here, this seat is more comfortable.'

Maolíosa sat on the edge of it. Regina had a bosom that an eleven-year-old would be absolutely sure to get a peep at. Certainly you should be able to see some of it, say from underneath the short summer sleeve, if she lifted one of her arms up, or definitely if she bent over to get something. God, what's got into me? Maolíosa wondered. Yesterday she had told a friend about a desperate craving for chocolate that had come over her recently.

'No I'm not, I'm not,' she said, annoyed at her friend's eyebrow which had shot up into a question mark. 'It's the spring, the summer, the sunshine, eating chocolate gives you a rush, a whoomph, like sex, we need it in the first flush of sun.'

'People know so much about themselves these days it takes the fun out of it.'

The room from where Miss Clarke worked was heavily wooden. The books and the old papers that were scattered on her desk had established their own smell. It had got into her, this smell of forever written descriptions of people's lives. The shelves were dark wood too. It was only this, the dark wood in the shelves, that saved the room from being the dispensary where Maolíosa had got her injections when she was a child. Come to think of it, Miss Clarke could have been the nurse, although you wouldn't be inclined to think about nipples if you were getting an injection.

'I just wanted to know how you started,' Maolíosa said.

'Well, I am prepared to discuss that, and that sort of thing, but nothing else really, because there are too many confidences at risk.'

'I understand that, Miss Clarke.'

'Regina.'

'Regina.'

'What's your name again?'

'Maolíosa.'

'Well, Maolíosa, I never wanted to start and although I've done this thing now for twenty-five years, mostly in my own time, I've never been paid a penny. But I don't mind. It was Jennifer really. She kept at me so much – surely I must be able to find out who her mother was – it's not possible that all trace of the original birth certs can't be found, surely it would do no harm, surely as a trusted employee I could get the birth certs, surely I must know after all these years how much she wanted to see her once, just once. And in the end I thought, well, I'll try, just to see for myself if I could find someone's mother, and a year later when I found her I thought, what harm could it do? What harm? So I went to her, Jennifer's mother, and she agreed, so for Jennifer's thirtieth birthday present I introduced her to her mother. I suppose the word spread after that. There's

a country full of them out there, and more again, much more
again, outside the country. They mostly come from England
now. But I don't meet those ones, they usually know the address by then, unless, of course, the mother has asked me from
this end, which is even dicier. Ah yes. Even dicier.'

Miss Clarke shuffled the papers.

'Ah yes, sometimes it can be very frightening. You know,
I've done a year or whatever of work and then they're meeting, having tea somewhere, and I'm at home wondering what
would happen if it all went wrong, if they killed each other or
something. I find myself always uneasy when there's a first
meeting on. Then, if one of them doesn't want to meet again
and one does, I sometimes think they might kill me, for the
address. Would you like a cup of tea?'

They had a cup of tea. Maolíosa spun yarns to herself about
how the editor would love this story. She saw promotion,
even heard voices saying, ask Maolíosa, she'd probably have
some ideas on that.

She went home knowing approximately how many people
had contacted Miss Clarke since the day the word got out that
she had found someone's mother. She knew how many were
male and female, what their general motivation was, how Miss
Clarke went about looking for their mothers. Miss Clarke always stressed that, first, the mother might be impossible to
find; second, she might not want to meet them (usually for fear
of her husband); third, she might be dead. If she found the
mother and the mother was agreeable, Miss Clarke set up a
meeting, after much advice to both not to expect too much
and not to whatever else was appropriate in the individual case.
You want to see some of the mothers that were mothers of
some of the people she met. It would make the hairs stand on
your head.

The room had got less like a dispensary as Miss Clarke

talked. Maolíosa had jotted down notes on scraps of paper, one case was even written on her hand. She had been reluctant to write too much or to take out a formal notebook because Miss Clarke eyed the pen and paper suspiciously. But she would sort it out now, spread mingy sentences on the desk and reshape them to give paper readers a sparse, undemanding picture of some thousands of secrets.

Cathal came home at twenty past five on the dot as usual. He was also supportive. In fact, he was god-damned nearly perfect. (Life must have been easy for him, thought Maolíosa, because she was driven to having some defence against his perfection.) She herself spent a lot of her time being irritable, being unsatisfied, being unreasonable. But life couldn't have been that easy for him. His parents had died five years ago, just before Maolíosa met him. He had no family, none at all. Surely that was hard, Maolíosa thought.

'She's really an interesting woman. Very unselfish. All that work for no money, no recognition. She can't even really tell anyone because in a sense it's breaking the spirit of adoption.'

'Perhaps she sees it as a hobby, your Miss Clarke.' He had taken an extraordinary dislike to Miss Clarke, he who never disliked anyone.

'Oh! Forget it, it doesn't really matter,' Maolíosa said, thinking that she might ruin the evening. He was entitled to his opinion. 'The article should be good anyway, although she won't let me meet any of the people concerned. Naturally, I suppose.'

'Your articles usually are. Probably a lot of unnecessary trouble though.'

'How did you get on today?' she thought it best to say.

And so they passed the evening, like any other, mostly in a pleasant way, a way founded on steadiness. The embarrassing, scarcely believable gymnastics of their first year were now an unshared memory that served only to prove, surely, their compatibility. Maolíosa supposed it was love that wove its way in and out between their sentences, their agreements, their apologies after their disagreements.

Sometimes Maolíosa looked at Cathal, like now, and noticed different things about him. Look – his moustache, it leaned to one side of his face as if it were a wind-beaten hedge, she'd never noticed that before. It was nice to know that there were new things. Oh Cathal, she thought, if we were younger we could be brother and sister and I would help you do your homework; here give me that, I'll do it for you, I've finished my own. Thanks. And then we'd grow up. I could leave. You wouldn't mind and I wouldn't mind, and you'd be there if I needed you.

Regina Clarke listened to the radio as she soaked in the bathroom. Tonight she was going out with her younger, ten years younger, brother. They had a proper night out once a month, not just because they were brother and sister but because they liked each other, enjoyed a lot of the same outings, could watch the embarrassing parts of the films as if they were either the most natural thing, so much so that they didn't deserve unease, or else so unnatural as to cause them no bother, because that carry-on couldn't be for real. He was a relief from herself at times, a light-hearted unworried person. Regina generally got through her days with a minimum of panic, but sometimes that job! Not her real job, the other one. Each attempted finding was a challenge. She could always cope with one expectant person, but when her trail was getting hot, and then hotter, she began to worry. Two people, now, linked through her – well, linked would be the wrong word, they were, after all, mother and child – dependent on her, to say yes or no way, no way, never. How will she tell that to another one?

'Your mother, taking all things into consideration, would prefer not . . .'

'I don't believe you, I don't believe you, you've led me on.'

She put more hot water in the bath, slid herself forward and soaked her head. Her thick brown curls straightened, her hair swam as if it had a life of its own, spread out like her heart did sometimes. Her heart which didn't always live the life that other people thought it was undergoing.

She could hear people whispering that she never married, some with sympathy coated with curiosity, but when she said it herself, 'I never married', it sounded more like an underground triumph. Once, she had been very taken over with a man. Lots of times, still, she was taken over for a few tipsy days. But nowadays her patience ran out of gusto and the tipsy days ran into hangovers before a week was past.

That man was a different story. It was twenty-five years ago. He had spent a number of years in America and so had acquired a certain amount of mystery and an even greater amount of warranted or unwarranted confidence – how were any of them to know what he had actually achieved out there? He had black hair, was born in Galway, and never told the whole truth. As soon as he was sure of her, which only took a few months, he flirted continuously. On the edge of her mind, she could feel the indignity of it. His flirting, always in company where she could be made to feel small, was like a wasp buzzing around near her ear, although she tried not to look as she swatted annoyance from her face.

One day he just flirted himself away. Her friends said afterwards she was 'far too good for him', but she never really minded him or the memory of him. These same friends fell into marriage one by one. Regina had watched just-married and about-to-be-married women converge around the latest ring – isn't it lovely, let me see, it's beautiful. She felt obscenity escaping in puffs from inside that circle. She could never crowd around a ring. The ones who had most adamantly complained about other new wives losing contact with their friends were the very ones who hid themselves in cupboards after their nuptials. 'God help them,' said Regina, when she thought about them, and got on with her job and her second job.

Some evenings when Regina was soaking she imagined her bath much bigger than it was, ten times larger at least, and there the important things of her life swam with her – a job well done; brisk Saturday mornings in the city turning languid, holding her there until afternoon; dinners; absolutely special words from men whom she had the nerve to leave; music evenings with her brother; her fine face. And the annoyances swam away.

Today she didn't do that because she must go out. The young woman who came was nice. She was coming again next week. She hurried to meet her brother. She always thought of him as her brother, not as Martin.

'No,' the editor said, 'it's not of sufficient interest.'

'That's not true,' Maolíosa said.

The editor had important diplomacies to consider, a story like that could upset a lot of people from all sides – his assistant editor, for instance, had an adopted child, this much he knew for definite. He was sure Maolíosa would question the morality of adoption in the surprised way she had. Sometimes he couldn't decide, and didn't really want to find out, if her surprise was genuine. She was good, but didn't understand words like 'necessity' or 'arrangement' or 'best suit'. How do you think his assistant editor would react? And who else was there in the office? You never knew. Why, you were never even sure about yourself.

Maolíosa left early. She stepped out into a shockingly spring day. I will do it. I will do it. So! So what if this stinking pompous fart doesn't want it. So what. She sighed because really she knew that all that rage blowing up like a balloon was simply an empty reassurance that she was getting somewhere in her job. And it was empty. Nothing ever came out on a page in that paper but the briefest glimpse of the truth. But I will do it, she thought, one whole story, or maybe small parts of several stories. I will write it down for a start.

She said to Cathal, exactly as he came in the door: 'Guess what? He won't even contemplate it.'

'Someone has sense.'

'I'm going to do something anyway. I feel a certain responsibility to those people.'

'That's nonsense. You don't even know any of them. It would suit you better to have responsibility to people you do know.'

'Oh well, it won't do any harm.'

'You think,' he said.

So when Maolíosa called to see Regina the following week it was with a different proposition.

'Let me meet some of the people or at least tell me some of the stories and I'll promise to keep their identities secret.'

'But what for?'

'I want to write a play maybe.' The idea of a play had only just struck her but it might be one way. 'With you as the central character.'

Regina Clarke smiled an altogether amused smile and yet a line pulled at her left eye. 'Ah, no.'

'But . . .'

Maolíosa was determined. She had been awake since dawn, plotting, enjoying the excitement of it. (Pity about Cathal's inexplicable antipathy.) She had planned the exposure of the real story, not the signing of the papers that complied with an act drawn up by a government – no, the real stories.

She cajoled Miss Clarke into daydreaming. Miss Clarke dreamt real worth into her life. Because she was engaged with such dynamite emotions – deciding to find your mother was hardly like buying a house – she sometimes had to believe that everyone else's life was such a trivial thing really. That way she could approach each search as if it didn't make a blind bit of difference whether or not this person ever met its mother. If she didn't do this, then they might all crack up under the nerves. But if everyone else's life, mother, was a trivial matter, your own wasn't – it was, well, it was life. Yours. Your one and only.

To tell or not to tell? She'd spent her life with these secrets, gone to bed with them, even forgotten some of them. But surely she did deserve something out of it. Truly her part in it was worth something. She had managed to calm people as they plunged through dangerous thoughts, she had even understood them – didn't she know that deciding to find your mother was hardly like buying a house? The government had never paid her, even though it helped them that she was doing this, took the pressure off them, so to speak. No one had ever paid her. Still, if she did tell, if she hinted a do-it-yourself find-your-mother method, then you might have hordes of people looking for their mothers, people turning up after Sunday dinner on unsuspecting doorsteps, mothers who were just about to take a nap, saying, 'Wait there a minute', nearly closing the door (you couldn't completely close the door on your own flesh and blood if they were actually standing there in front of you, rather than lying in a cot) and saying, 'John', or 'Peter', or 'Paddy', or 'Mick', 'Could you come here for a minute there's something I have to tell you.' The lucky ones would at least have a separate sitting room in which to drop the bombshell.

Could she tell her life story without dropping DIY hints?

Maolíosa talked on, piling up reasons why she should, and if they did it in some way different than a newspaper, they could have more scope, they could mix the names up. Colours of hair, hospitals, counties of origin, birth weight, could all be swapped around.

It was the sound of Maolíosa's voice that did the trick, Miss Clarke had to say to herself afterwards, because suddenly a certain mischief took her over and shook her like you would a thing you wanted to put life into and she said, 'Why not, what harm could it do?'

And so the next six months were spent delving in and out of stories. Sometimes in Regina's office, overlooking the canal and the ducks.

'What do you mean the mother was married when she had it? But I thought . . .'

Maolíosa was confident here now. Once, when sitting on the desk, she caught herself staring at Regina's V-necked dress. That thing they call a cleavage – it was like a crease, a watershed, the down shape of any single thing thrown in a heap – why was it so breathtaking? It was as if that line was the piercing needle of the body below. Had Miss Clarke had many, any, orgasms? Regina was judging her this evening, she was sure. Sometimes she was friendly, but sometimes she looked down her nose at Maolíosa, bragging years. Maolíosa was still young enough to hate that. Did Miss Clarke have many orgasms? Maolíosa rubbed her ankle against the desk leg to bring back the conversation they'd been having. What business of hers was it anyway?

Other times they met in Regina's house. It was a severe semi-detached house, one of those places that could never have been part of anybody's plan, how could it? A blank, faceless transfer, that might crop up in a nightmare somewhere. Everyone on the street was married, except Regina. The husbands all earned the same money, the wives had all stopped work at the same time, done prenatal classes together, decided there was no need for their husbands to be there when the births would happen (that way they could have an extra day's holiday when the wives would be able to enjoy their company), discussed birth control, and had second children within three months of each other. Regina's brother had seen the house on his way home from work. They went to see it together. When they turned into the street, Regina gasped, 'What are you trying to do to me? A street like this! You'd have me out here surrounded by Mr and Mrs, people washing cars and mowing lawns.'

But inside, the house was different, different enough to show how even more different it could be. And now it was. For such a young and correct house, it held the old furniture, the strewn records, the dust, with unexpected style. It had made the bathroom its own, the enormous bath, the foams, the smells. The bathroom jolted Maolíosa, the first time. It was such a warm, well, warm and wet, bathroom that she was embarrassed. Imagine Miss Clarke. Ah! Just imagine.

And then when Cathal wasn't there they met in Maolíosa's flat, one window of which looked out on other windows and a series of scorched gardens. Regina liked the austerity of the few unmatched pieces of furniture. Maolíosa and Cathal never accumulated enough money to get a set of anything, not even of cups.

In these three places, with their different furnitures, their different views, Maolíosa and Regina began to write down the facts. But first the stories, and some of them Maolíosa would have to meet herself. Regina would tell her who she could meet, fix it up in some pleasant place. All part of their adventure. Where there were no proven words, Maolíosa imagined sentences, conversations, between the pregnant women and the men.

THE MEEK

'The band was good.'

He wasn't sure: 'From where we were you couldn't see them.'

'Frank, I'm going to have a baby.'

'Jesus Christ.'

THE EXPECTING THE WORST

'Could I speak to Mr Hogan, please?'

'May I ask who is calling?'

'It's personal.'

'Eamon, I have to tell you now, it's easier by telephone, I'm pregnant.'

'Jesus Christ.'

THE JAUNTY AND CONFIDENT

'Guess what?'

'What?'

'We're going to have a baby.'

'Jesus Christ.'

THE TERRIFIED

'They'll kill me. I'm pregnant.'

'Jesus Christ.'

Yes, Jesus Christ. The country was a garden full of virgin births. And then there were the blanks where no conversation had taken place at all because there was no point, or she knew the answer anyway and wouldn't humiliate herself further, or she was too embarrassed because she didn't know him well enough, or this would be his excuse to force a wedding on her and in no time she'd be up to her neck in muck and his life.

Maolíosa and Regina lifted their sadness sometimes by

concentrating on the mischief they were doing. They were blowing bits out of the bottom of the rock.

'No, I don't want her to find me. How could I look her in the eye? I abandoned her. I hope she's been happy and that they were good to her. Why? Why did I do it? Because, because I was told to, that's why. My parents are now in heaven, no doubt, with the rest of them.'

The woman's eyes were hollow. She was tall and see-through thin. She wore her tailored, expensive clothes easily, because she was used to them all her life but she didn't get any comfort from such good material. The clothes themselves would have given the world to be worn with delight.

'Actually, I do want her to find me, maybe she would forgive me.'

Aoife had changed her name to Eva, it sounded more important. She was tall and happily thin. She didn't care beyond the next customer in the nightclub, the next good-looking customer that is. She was going to London next week, where you can get jobs like these in the *daytime*, all day long – winebars. Winebars everywhere. Two of her friends from the orphanage were already there (there had never been any 'they' to be good to her). One of them was getting her a job. No, she didn't care whether or not she ever saw her mother, she knew others that had done it and it wasn't *good* for them. Much too risky meeting your mother, you wouldn't know *what* she'd be like. She could be any one of a thousand kinds of person. Eva knew all the types that came to nightclubs, and you mightn't like *anything* about her. It would be nice, though, if she was *stinking* rich, but there was no guarantee that she'd give any of it to *her*, so far, she hadn't actually fallen about the place proving how much she loved her. No, it wouldn't be a good idea –

one of her friends went to see her mother and the biggest shock
was that there were three children who looked *exactly*, I mean
exactly, like herself. So did the mother. It was spooky, her not
being used to seeing people that looked in any way like her. I
tell you, it was spooky. No, she was going to London next
week so she wouldn't have time anyway.

Maolíosa dreamed about the two of them. She couldn't bear
that she knew something they didn't know. The dream
choked in her mouth, making it smell of vomit. But in the
morning she forced herself to accept that they had no daily
worries about the matter. The mother had a simple, everlasting, unattainable desire to be forgiven but she didn't think
about it all the time. It was just there, like a medium bad back-
ache. And even if her daughter did forgive her, it would still be
there. The daughter had no desire whatever to have her curiosity stirred up. She had grown up with her peers. Old people,
like mothers, weren't that important, they were just like the
nuns at the orphanage. The last thing mother and child
needed was Maolíosa with her caring and her bloody good
will.

Regina said, oh, that's nothing. But she knew how Maolíosa felt. She'd get immune though, just like undertakers do.
Presumably the first funeral was always the worst. She was also
afraid, because if Maolíosa started pointing out these things,
would it not remind her of each and every case? How many
times had she looked out at that canal? They always sat down
for a few minutes before they came in to her. Naturally, she
supposed, it was a big step. They always stared at the ducks.
Young women, young men, middle-aged women. One
middle-aged woman, middle of what age? Regina remembered her. She had looked out the window and saw her staring
at the ducks and knew that that must be Mrs Coyle. She had a

dark brown scarf with a horse's head on it – a big wide head, big open eyes, and a speck of brown on its forehead. Around the edge of the scarf the smaller horses' heads looked out satisfiedly at passers-by as if it was the most natural place to be. One of the horses' heads was mangled in the knot tied under Mrs Coyle's chin. Another peeped over Mrs Coyle's shoulder and also stared at the ducks.

Mrs Coyle explained: 'Birthdays have always been bad but this one finished me. It didn't go away after the day was over. Every day now is his birthday. I have to do something.' She was falling in inside, landslides were tearing away from her heart and dropping into her stomach. His birthday had a hold on her face and was pinching it. 'You have to help me or I will die, I really will die.'

His birthday might kill her. Regina asked her about her husband, as she usually did, but this time she particularly meant it because someone would have to be told about this poor woman's heart.

'My husband is very good, very kind, oh, he's a wonderful husband.'

'Well, would you not perhaps tell him then?'

Mrs Coyle thought it a pity, considering. Considering what? Well, she said shyly, when she was having him the doctor said he'd have to do a section. But there was one other thing they could do instead of a section and it wouldn't leave a scar in case she ever got married and didn't want her husband to know and would she prefer that? And she said, yes, she would prefer that. They broke her pelvis – it seemed like they did it with a saw – a hammer or a saw.

Regina bit her lip and involuntarily held on to her pubic bone the way men grab their balls during a free kick.

Because of going through all that, it had seemed silly to tell him at first and then a month was a year and a half-truth became a half-lie and then a year was five years and she had her 'first' child, and a half-lie became such a monstrous untruth that it didn't bear thinking about. And now his birthday had got her.

Regina met Mrs Coyle often in the next six months and these meetings kept Mrs Coyle from dying. In the end she told her husband because there didn't seem anything else she could do because she had stopped sleeping. The pinch went out of her face. He took it like a gentleman but it diminished certainty for him. And yet he got something from the 'announcement', as he henceforth called his wife's squeezed sentences. He had been picked to be one of the men who married women who had secretly had children before their weddings. It did something for him. He then came with Mrs Coyle to see Regina.

Regina found Mrs Coyle's son, a fair-haired young man, who seldom smiled and even when he did his face remained flat. He was delighted. They all met, and that should have been the end of that. But one day Mrs Coyle turned up again. She had hurried frantically past the ducks.

'He wants to know who his father is. He's very insistent. Is that normal?'

'Well, does your husband know?'

'He never asked. I suppose he thought it improper. And I never told him, I thought that it would make it too real. You see everything is real, once I've told it to him.'

Regina said that Mrs Coyle would have to decide for herself.

The next day Mrs Coyle stood waiting for the shop to open in her village and decided. It would all have to be told now and she put her hand to her throat. Her husband's boss. His mealy-mouthed, snide, know-all boss. God help us, it would all have to be told now.

★

Regina felt sorry to have held one over on Maolíosa.

'I didn't really mean that it was nothing,' she said. 'Here, do you need any carpet? Remember the man I told you about last week? He's just met his mother, he's forty-five. Well, his friend works on the ships, maintaining them, and apparently they often remove all the carpet from the ships even though only some of it is worn and he said that if ever I wanted any, to give him a shout. It is always the one colour, red, blue or green.'

'Oh great, we certainly could do with a carpet.'

They needed more than a new carpet, Maolíosa thought.

There had been an awful row. Maolíosa still had a headache. She had come home. She had smiled at Cathal and then told him about the woman she'd met, an acquaintance of Regina's brother, who wanted to help, because she had never quite re-covered from her brush with 'that kind of thing'. Maolíosa knew that Cathal hated these interviews but she didn't know the seriousness of why. Anyway, she had to tell someone. The woman today wondered what life was like now for the woman who had been in the bed beside her.

'I remember she told me that she was an alcoholic. I said that she couldn't be, not at nineteen, but then the visitors came from AA so she must have been. She said she never remem-bered getting pregnant – maybe she did but couldn't admit it. She was giving the baby up. Up to where? I used to think as we both lay, trying not to disturb our stitches. "They say if I keep it I'll only go back on the drink." "Who are they?" "The friends from AA and my mother" (who had come sneakily on her own, supposedly going for a check on her varicose veins, and never looked at the child once). "They say! They say! But what do you say, Linda, what do you say?" "Well, I know one thing, I'm not taking it out of that basket. It's not fair to expect me to do anything with it. I'm giving it up, amn't I? The nurses can change its nappy." And I began to feel privileged to wash the shit from around my baby's bottom. I put my nipple into my baby's mouth, touching his cheek with it first so he snuggled his mouth, round and open, burying his nose in my breast.

'My baby drank guilt, as I could see from the corner of my eye Linda's basket untouched, writhing instead of rocking between the bedposts where it was hung, sending screeches up and up, its mother with stone for a face, and then a nurse would come. "Now Linda," she would say, "you know it's best if you get to know it. Then you won't feel later that you had no choice." "I'm not touching that basket." And there I was, allowed to feed my baby with my very own nipple because I could take it home, because a man had asked me to marry him and I had said yes, or maybe I had asked him. "Think of anything," I whispered to my baby, as inconspicuously as I could manage. When Linda left the ward I always picked him up and squeezed him properly and then I would go to Linda's basket where I would lay my fingers on her child's head and say some tight useless cliché.

'Forty-eight hours after Linda and I had pushed our babies out, I turned on my left side and saw her move towards her basket. She leaned up on her hunkers, then thought better of it, moved again, then back. There was a god playing with her to see how much magnet she was. She got down from the bed carefully and pulled herself ghostlike to the basket. She dug her hands into it, clenching her eyes, and came out with a baby. She seemed surprised at it, then kissed it full on the mouth. I heard her whisper as if the words were escaping from her. So from then on my baby drank tears and apprehension because Linda would not leave her baby out of her arms even when the nurses said, "Come on now, it needs to sleep; come on, you need to sleep." "I can sleep all I like later," she said.

'I asked to be let out a few hours early because I hadn't the stomach to watch the passing over of Linda's baby to an intermediary, who would then pass it over to some married infertile couple. That's how I came to leave the hospital on a Sunday morning instead of a Sunday evening.'

When Maolíosa told Cathal what the woman had said, there had been the terrible row. Cathal had been like a mad man. And Maolíosa, after she had cried away all her rage at him, gave up the interviews, the talks and Regina.

The news came on, Maolíosa and Cathal smiled at each other. They didn't always look at each other over breakfast but when they caught each other's eyes on the way up for more toast, or on the way down to drink more tea, they smiled. A smile that had everlasting written on it because if, as well as being totally loyal, they could do for each other and themselves what they had done last night, with the covers thrown back, then everlasting must surely be on the cards. The news reader said: 'The new Children's Bill which does away with the status of illegitimacy comes before the Dáil today. There will be no more Nobody's Child.'

'Christ,' Maolíosa said, 'they never *were* nobody's child, they were their mothers' children, surely.'

But Cathal turned off the radio. A flash, like the snarl of a dog, passed over his lips and eyes, but there he now was, smiling again, Maolíosa would have to split herself a little. Last nights should be better nurtured. They should have put music on, not the news. Her headache was back. And the row started again. 'I've given up doing the interviews, what more do you want?' The day was ruined.

Cathal imagined himself running into a river and forgetting how to swim. He could leave, couldn't he? But he couldn't leave all this. This for him was the whole of it. Someone to talk to in the evening, every evening, the sound of her feet in bedroom slippers dragging as in a slow dance around the kitch-en when it was her turn to cook breakfast on a Saturday morn-ing. This was the plug that stopped a deluge from falling on his head. But now he was dreaming every night that a river was coming towards him from the other direction. Yet last night he had woken in a cold sweat and found himself lying peace-fully. The front of his right foot lay curled on the back of her left foot, for all the world like a lover who had decided.

Maolíosa put order on the shelves, the toilet, the bedclothes. She walked out, pleased with such tidiness. In the bank she no-ticed a man whom she'd last noticed two years ago. He had got older, got settled. She remembered him as a young boy. He looked over all the bank now with confidence – when she first noticed him he had kept his eyes down and only looked at a desk or another clerk when he was standing right beside it or them. He seemed to be growing into the bank, he even had the nerve now to wear a slightly creased shirt. How could anyone be expected to spend their life on that one side of a counter, being stared at mechanically by customers? Were they very nice to him when he had a hangover? He must have hang-overs, he now had a drink belly. So clean, God they were all so clean. They had to wash the smell of sex off themselves every morning – you couldn't have them smelling like that in a bank and especially not when the desks were so near each other and the canteen was so small. Pity that – because smel-ling the smell next morning was often the best part, letting it waft up in the middle of your stomach and through the nose to your brain, which did the remembering, the reconstruction, and made you feel all randy again.

She left the bank, upset by the sight of the young man growing into the bank walls. What was she going to do now? There was a burning above her legs, and an aggravating tic in her brain telling her to leave, leave everything, free herself,

spread her wings. It was not good enough to spend your life
with one man. Especially when he had become so cantan-
kerous. It was not good enough that she got enormous pleasure from tidying shelves. And yet when her job took her
away she thought all the time of her one man. Even more so
if she was in bed with somebody else – her eyes filled up with
tears at the thought of such simple pleasure. Once a man was
the someone else it meant he was new, exciting, took his time,
looked at her maybe, worked his way up to her very womb,
and grinned with surprise at her lack of inhibition. But what
would she do without her one man, what would happen between five and ten in the evening? She would drink too much,
go to bed with too many unsuitable men who only needed a
tight body to wrap around their pricks in order to make mas-
turbation easier. But then she might also lie down beside a
stranger and they might drink each other's very breath, staring
deep down to the backs of their eyes, touching their fingers
over each other's lips, while they joined the bottom part of
their bodies together, pretending that they were doing nothing
more that putting two parts of a jigsaw together, until their
eyes became dim, misted over, their smiles became a little
pained and they devoured each other like wolves, screaming
love, sex, betrayal, emptiness, fullness and pleasure, as they
kissed each other's cheekbones afterwards. Why did sex make
such a different thing of friendship? Oh well, it did, thank
God, thank God.

Regina went for a walk. She would meet her brother and his
friend at seven. They were to have a meal. She had no curiosity
about her brother's friend. She might have had, but she was
too preoccupied with disappointment. She hadn't believed
that Maolíosa would drop the venture so completely. Because
she thought Maolíosa stronger than that. That's couples for

you, she tried hard not to sneer. She walked over Charlemont Street bridge and looked down on a duck sliding into the water. It gave a back wave of its foot, a dismissive wave, kicking the water away without a ripple. Well, if you're worried, it's your problem, you don't seriously expect me to take on the pain of every fool that stares at me? I'd be dead long ago of worried duck disease if I did that. It gave another wave. Point taken, Regina said, and walked on. Saturday is couples day around Grafton Street, they were everywhere, fighting and kissing. I suppose Maolíosa and Cathal are among them. They won't be fighting now because he got his way. She walked behind a man, woman and child. The man and woman seemed to pursue each other, because although she was a few steps in front of him, her comments seemed to be directed at his back.

'You're as thick as two short planks.'

Regina thought that a funny thing for a woman dressed like her to say.

He said, 'A small zip on your mouth wouldn't go astray.'

She said, 'If you wanted to be an actor, why didn't you join the Abbey?'

He said, 'God preserve me from your ignorance, that's all I ask.'

The child ignored them. It could have slipped away unnoticed. Couples, Regina sniffed, and turned into another street.

Another child was having its day. It said, sure and clear, 'I love the sound of my daddy's voice.'

Regina was startled and turned to look at such a child. That was obviously her daddy. He was beaming. Certainly. Always as soon as Regina had couples relegated they started kissing, even the sedate ones in bristly woollen jumpers. That was her luck with dismissiveness. But really, Maolíosa should have been stronger. After all the work they both had done, not to talk of Regina's whole life, but, of course, Maolíosa was a little young, acted too surprised at times, was too surprised. Acted beaten at times, was beaten.

'That was particularly difficult. The mother had been forced to give it up. It seems the father was a priest,' Regina said.

Maolíosa said, 'If you had published that, there would have been an uproar. An absolute uproar.'

'No, I don't think so. It's not what is uncovered and said openly that matters, it's who says it.'

Maolíosa had looked beaten.

When Regina had explained the procedure for making out the new birth certificate for the adopted child, Maolíosa had said, astonished, 'But that's illegal. Completely illegal. A birth certificate says who your parents are. Well, who you came from. You can't just go and change it. It's illegal.'

'Of course it's illegal,' Regina almost snapped, annoyed at Maolíosa's honest bafflement.

'Birth certificates are a complete insult to mothers anyway. They're all about the fathers,' Maolíosa said.

'That's nothing to do with us.'

Maolíosa had looked both surprised and beaten. She was too young. But so resilient. She would call again when the trouble with Cathal had blown over. Of course she would. Regina had better go home, have her bath, and meet her brother.

Months passed as months will. Other things happened to Regina, Cathal and Maolíosa. They ate, slept, worked, walked, ran for buses, read newspapers. But other things were really just padding. All three had, in different ways, been linked on a roller coaster. They knew that this would not be the end of them, could not be the end of this. Regina waited with patience because she was sure. Other things happened but they weren't important.

★

Maolíosa was twiddling her laces, hugging her knees, closing her eyes tight to stop herself from crying. Come on, come on, crying will only be temporary relief, it won't solve anything. Answer the questions, Maolíosa, she said sternly to herself. She had divided them into single questions rather than one big unruly one. What am I going to do? Why is Cathal so impossible? Has he got tired of me? What am I going to do? What would he say if I said I was leaving? And then, in case he'd say, well, all right, she thought, oh don't be silly, I'm not going to say that. Of course I'm staying. I'm staying because I want to stay, he's just out of sorts. It must have been all that talk about children and parents. His own parents were dead, she would have to remind herself of that again. Funny how you could forget the biggest thing about other people's lives just because your own mother was still there somewhere to run to. I'm sorry, Cathal, sorry, but I'll have to make up my mind, for you, for me. Oh I'll stay, my love, I'll stay. Could I let him go? No. But it would surely be better than this recurring politeness that festers into torrents of gall every chance he gets. I could let him go because I'd have to, because he's mine no more than he's anyone else's. I couldn't help him pack, nor could I give him a train or taxi fare, nor kiss him goodbye, nor wish him good luck, but if I had to . . . I couldn't allow myself to think of someone else touching his face, some stranger unbuttoning his shirt, him ringing up a telephone number belonging to some complete and utter drop-in, some pointless nobody, but if I had to . . . I think I will ask him.

But she didn't ask him, as such. She said in a low voice in reaction to one more sniping hour, 'Either I go or you tell me what's got into you.'

She waited for him to say, Well, go then. Instead he looked at her with eyes that were like death. She had not noticed how black they had become. They startled her.

'Because my parents are not dead. I am one of your precious adopted children. I do not know who my parents are. Yes, I was reared by two people who tried to make me believe that it doesn't matter. For that ignorance I hate them and buried them the day I left what they so presumptuously call home.'

He put the kettle on and looked a little amused. He was terribly relieved. The black went from his eyes and soaked into Maolíosa's skin, making her grey.

Maolíosa stayed grey for a week, her hands shook a lot; she felt a little afraid of Cathal, of someone who could have told such a lie. But then they moved closer to each other, stripped each other's faces and ran their tongues over each other's lips. They would go to see his adoptive parents, of course she would go with him, but first they would find his real mother and then he would feel better.

Regina was surprised when both Cathal and Maolíosa arrived on her doorstep; she had expected only Maolíosa.

When the day came for Cathal to meet his mother, Maolíosa chose the clothes that she thought he should wear. Cathal wanted Maolíosa to be with him, so she dressed in a grey blouse, a pair of black linen trousers, and her good jacket, which she had got from the cleaners just in time before they closed for the weekend. Phew! She talked about lots of emergencies like this in order to distract him, and her. He wore dark green cord trousers, a faintly tinted loose silk shirt and a new jacket that had cost Maolíosa nearly the earth. He looked lovely.

They were meeting on a Saturday. Cathal and his mother would spend half an hour together first, then they would join Maolíosa in the foyer of Buswell's Hotel, they would have a drink, well, they didn't know whether she drank or not, maybe she totally disapproved, stop being nervous, Cathal, it

will be all right, maybe she won't like the idea of us living together, well, she can hardly object, Maolíosa tittered, and
knew that that was a terrible thing to say but you had to laugh
all the same, then they would go for a meal and it will be all
right, Cathal, stop fretting.

Afterwards what shocked Maolíosa most was how well
they all had handled it. All of them. Maolíosa was sitting, trying to watch the door without looking at it. Cathal came in, he
looked only a little nervous. Maolíosa stood up. But the
woman with him was Maolíosa's mother. As far as Maolíosa
could remember, she and her mother dropped their mouths
open together and then put their hands over their eyes in uni-
son, pretending that they were fixing their hair, wishing that
they could draw all reality into that space between their eyes
and the palms of their hands. That way, it could harm no
one. They reached blindly for their seats, her mother less
blindly than her. Cathal looked at them for a long minute before he realised. He hit the side of his head with an index finger
that had jammed stiff as iron and also reached for a seat. They
all had brandy.

'I suspected, only for a minute, that it was you,' Maolíosa's
mother said to her. 'Once, when Miss Clarke was talking to
me, but I thought it simply couldn't be possible. I suspected
again when I met' – she floundered her hand – 'this young
man, but by then it was too late. Better to face it now than
when you would bring him home to see us.'

She fixed her eyes then on an infinite point behind their
heads and made her plea. She didn't ask Cathal, nor Maolíosa
for that matter, for forgiveness; Maolíosa thought later, wasn't
that strange, wasn't that brave of her really? She spoke in a
voice that Maolíosa had never heard before.

'How could I have thought that I could have him for keeps?
A man like that could give me the nerve to look through him,

right down into his eyes – as if I were above him – past his big heart, hesitating for as long as I could manage without being blinded, and the smooth silk stomach of him and then say, can I hold you, can I really put you inside me? And him to say, oh yes, oh yes, any time, any time. I had known slaps on the face and news of another war, how could I have thought that my time had come? All the while that I was licking across his tongue, ice-cream-eating fashion, and sliding me down so that the tip of him would fill my heart, he must have been looking over my shoulder for others to whom he would give nerve. He liked giving nerve as a gift. So when I found a little of him growing where he had been, my heart was already closed. I couldn't look at a child like him when I would never now have him. How could I? How could I? Don't look at me like that, please. You should understand. Maybe not, maybe not, maybe you've never loved a man like I loved him. Isn't it a strange thing, then, you've never loved this boy like I loved . . .?

Her voice tapered into the silence.

She refused another brandy, the train was going soon. She left quite steady-footed. Cathal and Maolíosa had one more brandy each and then they walked home together, holding hands, shaking a little at their knees.

Regina Clarke is now paid by the government to find people's mothers.

PETTY CRIME

All children should have a letter from their father to their mother that they can find some day when they're rooting through boxes looking for something else. This is Brendan Gaffney's children's letter. That is, if their mother doesn't tear it up or burn it. He felt a little seedy writing it, sitting there in the waiting room of the North Wall, watching out from under his eyebrows for the opening of the doors of the Liverpool boat. Seedy, because he knew that he was writing it not just for Mags and the children but also because it made him look innocent. No man running away would be sitting writing a letter. He'd be more likely to be talking to someone, a stranger even, so that he wouldn't look conspicuous, or reading a paper. The *Irish Times*. Criminals don't read the *Irish Times*, not small-time ones anyway. Seedy and something else as well, a man with the bottom knocked out of him, but that's so big to think about, it couldn't be thought about. He looked at his shoes, they were as clean as anything.

Dear Mags,
By the time you get this I'll be safely in Liverpool or somewhere. I'll let you know as soon as I get an address. I know this will upset you but there was nothing else I could have done . . .

Brendan had not always been destined to be skulking away in the early night. Sixteen years ago he and Margaret Daly married; they went to Las Palmas for their honeymoon and didn't really like it. The first week was OK but the second dragged a bit. If it hadn't been for a couple from Kerry, also on their honeymoon, they would have gone mad.

Part of the reason that the week dragged was because they were dying to get home, home to this great new house which the firm Brendan worked for had almost finished. Because the house was for Brendan, the lads had done all sorts of little extra things, things they had hauled up from the bottoms of their imaginations, brass fittings on the doors, a serving hatch between the kitchen and the dining room, 'For when there's hundreds of little Gaffneys, Brendan, hundreds ...' And the bedroom! You could sleep in the wardrobe and still there was space for a dressing table, a bedside locker, which the lads had bought for them, guffawing for days afterwards, and the bed. Their bed, where they could stay on a Sunday morning; indeed, they could stay in it all day Sunday, as long as they pulled the curtains open at some reasonable hour. Mags's mother had said that there was great liberty in the house. He liked Mags's mother.

In the beginning the years had gone in so satisfactorily it was a pity to see them go in at all, but if they hadn't, then the great days wouldn't have happened, so Mags and Brendan accepted the frizzling up of time. A day was a day and you couldn't expect anything more from it. The children were born, looked lovely and began to turn out well.

But two years ago, steady work became a thing of history and Brendan's ease began to wobble. It was just at the time when the children seemed to be costing more, the mortgage had gone up, the house needed to be painted, some of the gutters needed repairing, Mags had to have her teeth done – if she

didn't have them done now, they'd fall out – the school tours
cost a fortune. Every second year half the classes in the school
went on a major tour. Their children were all two years apart.
If they hadn't planned so well, the school tours wouldn't have
cost so much. That year it was Chester, Paris and Russia. And
somehow, between one thing and the other, that year became
their lives, that year became nothing more than a scramble to
the surface to gasp for air. They kept their mouths open as
wide as possible when they breathed in. The Christmas presents, one bicycle, one computer, one music-maker, finished
them off completely.

The slither down to poverty has no music to go with it. It's
not a thing that can be portrayed by a loud thunderous clang, a
steady march, a mournful sonata. It is too unobvious, it takes
too long, it is too unpretty. Brendan began to make lists in his
head and say them out loud. The lists nearly drove him mad.
On good days they were about getting on with it. On bad days
they were, well, bad. He would have done some work on the
house but the list of what it would cost didn't balance the pros.
Despite all this, sometimes Mags and he folded into each other
as if there were paid bills cramming every drawer in the house.
Those times made the next day smell of spring, but it was always spring before winter.

Uinseann McGrath called at six o'clock one Wednesday to
tell Brendan that there was two days' work on a job at the top
of Rathmines. Finishing job, all the renovation gear is there and
you'd never know, the builder might be good for more, he has
work all over the place. Brendan went down to Rory to tell
him that there was work in it for him too, mixing, but Rory
said no thanks. 'That's a mug's game,' he said, 'working your
arse off as if it was going to last. Not for me, Brendan, I've a
sideline on now. Come to think of it, I could get you ready cash
any time.' So Brendan gave the work to Joe Sweeney instead.

It wasn't a proper building site. There was no foreman with a sheepskin coat and the woman of the house was there. Before they had even started, she made them tea and gave them Kylemore jam doughnuts. She chatted to her husband across the table while they all ate together, the electrician, an eel of a man, and his docile helper, the labourers, one of them who wore uncouthness like an emblem, the plumber, sleazed to exhaustion, the roofer, who had a toothache. She talked about the day's work ahead – the board finish, the bonding, the skim beads, the twelve-foot lengths, the Wavin pipe and three-quarter-inch fittings, that new plastic piping and fascia board.

'Skim beads, you could never have enough of them,' Brendan said.

'Lead's your only man,' the roofer said by way of reply, worrying that she might see to Brendan's needs before his.

The woman talked as if the table was not sitting on the only part of the floor which was not a hole, as if there wasn't dust ground into every square inch around her, including the mugs and the teapot, as if there were windows in her house, as if there were walls and ceilings and doors, as if the bath wasn't sitting in the middle of the kitchen floor, gradually being broken, as passing tradesmen dropped tools on it, as if she and her husband would get over this some day.

Brendan started working. He was attended rhythmically, silently, by his helper. Joe Sweeney brought the right mixture with the right consistency at the right time. They were like dancers. Brendan plastered the walls, sprinkling them first. He twisted his wrist and threw as a man would sowing corn from a bag tied around his neck. He spread and plastered with lavish sweeping motions, rushing here and to that spot there, swiping unevenness off the face of the wall, tiptoeing then and brushing quietly, smoothing over the jaggedness as in the last waltz, before moving on to the next patch to start again. He loved working. He was still the best plasterer he'd ever met – he'd never forgotten a thing that was worth remembering about the job. He smelled the smell of building. Funny how you notice things when you're not with them every day. One of the labourers, the quiet one, finished some tricky job and leaned over it admiringly, 'Handy as a wee cunt,' he said, and Brendan hoped that the woman didn't overhear, but he saw her smiling a private smile.

They had tuna, peeled tomatoes, lettuce, eggs, cheddar cheese and scallions mixed on brown bread for lunch. Brendan knew that the tomatoes were peeled because Mags had shown him what a difference that makes to the texture of a sandwich. Would the woman of the house keep up this standard right through the job?

He went back to work, appraising first what he had already done. He fitted the skim bead in one movement and ran his hand down over it. This was spring before summer. He was paid in cash that evening, the notes were like silk handkerchiefs between his fingers.

The following morning Mags said, 'It's Chris's birthday next week. Get him some small thing. Just some small anything. A crossword book maybe or some small thing.'

Brendan thought, for God's sake I have only two days' work. He could feel his fury breaking inside him. It started in his stomach, went up into a word that spattered into more words, it went into a sneer, it turned the volume up on his bile, it put music to his rage – now that's something that does have its own symphony – it screamed at her stupidity, it banged its flat hand on the table, bouncing dishes up and down. He swallowed and never said a word. It wasn't her fault. The swallow tasted of razor blades.

'Are you all right? You look pale,' Mags said.

'Grand, no I'm grand.' He went to work and because he was

such a good plasterer he finished in one and three-quarter days instead of two. Less pay.

Brendan walked to the bus stop, he would get an 83 outside Hynes's. The guards used to drink in there when it was O'Byrne's. It was a furtive, smirched place then. He and Mags had drunk there sometimes when they were going out, if they couldn't get a seat in Slattery's or in the public bar in Madigan's. They wouldn't have been caught dead in the lounge in Madigan's. The Fine Gael Party met there, which was bad, but if they weren't there, it was worse, because everyone could hear every word you said. There were guards in there too. Why should Brendan worry about guards? He had never broken the law in his life nor did he intend to.

The 83 struggled down Rathmines Road. Brendan slipped along with it, remembering when names of streets and pubs used to mean something definite to him. A change in roofs, a peculiar shape to a window or a glimpse of a side street – he used to notice these things. In Georges Street he saw a shop's tactless boast – LIQUIDATION SHOP. CUSTOMERS WANTED. NO EXPERIENCE NECESSARY. He got off at the next stop; maybe he could get something for Chris there, something cheap that would have been dearer in better times. He waded through pots and pans, crockery, screwdrivers, hotwater bottles, getting dizzy. There wasn't a damn thing you could buy for a child. He came out and leaned against the litter bin; he had a stitch in his side and he had wasted a bus fare.

Now let's see that list again. Outgoings against incomings. Mortgage: dole. Bus fares: dribs and drabs from the EHB. Food: Children's Allowance. The phone was gone. They hadn't had a car for three years, although Mags, always the optimist, kept the licence renewed. The three pound that Joe pays him back from that loan he gave him years ago. An odd drink, and how come it tastes better now than it ever had? One sip of the first and he wants a second. Once he's ordered the second, he craves for a third. He had never been a big drinker. When it came to the third, one of the men would say, 'Brendan'll be goin' now, home to the missus, can't get enough of her.' Hey, Brendan. Hey, Brendan. Now, say if the mortgage went down and the Children's Allowance went up and they did all their shopping at Crazy Prices in one swipe and he asked Joe for more than three pound towards the debt and say . . .

'Taking a rest Brendan?' Rory said, clapping him on the back, sending the pain scattering through him.

'Remember what you said about that sideline? Well, if anything comes up . . .' There. He'd said it.

'Certainly, Brendan, certainly.'

Rory called at his house a few weeks later. He was pale and jumpy. He wanted Brendan to do something urgently. Luckily Mags was out. A young fellow had taken a shot.

'I don't want to know nothing,' Brendan said.

'There's a few hundred in it for you. A good few. All you have to do is collect the doctor from James's Hospital. It's all arranged with her. You'll be given a car.'

'Right,' Brendan said.

Mags came back. He left with Rory in Rory's car. No problem with that – they were going to price a job.

Brendan tried to remember which streets they were going through. He would have to remember his way back, he would just have to. In the flat, two men plastered make-up on his face. It made him as inconspicuous as a lighthouse, but he had to believe that they knew what they were doing. When they brought him to the car, he doubted it. The back window was broken. It looked for all the world as if it had been stolen within the last hour. Dear God, please no. The bloody back window was broken. Steady, he said there's a few hundred pound in it. A good few. What's a few? What's a good few?

'Good' was a word he was never sure of. He reached in and cleared the jagged pieces of glass, not daring to look over his shoulder.

He drove stiffly. The make-up on his face began to run down his neck, but he was afraid to wipe it away. A sliver of early March sun glaring through the windscreen wasn't helping. Only good thing about that, a sunny morning made the back window less noticeable. Two women crossed the road, gesticulating to high heavens; he could imagine them taking off in one of those gestures. It was so ordinary, so secure, one of them put her hand on her heart. Mags does that and says honest to God at the same time. He had to slam on the brakes or he would have hit them. They turned faces ferociously to him and one of them puckered curiously. He sped away.

The doctor got into the back of the car nonchalantly. She sat behind him as if she did this every day of the week. It calmed Brendan down. There was nothing wrong with what he was doing, a work of mercy, never mind the money. I'm with the doctor, that would cover a person for anything. He hoped she wouldn't notice the make-up caking now behind his ears. He found the right block of flats, and the right hall and the right number. He tapped twice casually with the back of his hand. The man who had brought him to the car opened the door and let them in. He left Brendan standing in the hallway and brought the doctor into the kitchen. There was no sign of Rory. Brendan stood in the narrow hallway, stiff again with fear, listening to the doctor's quiet voice. How long would it take her? She was out again in what seemed like a minute.

'Are you done?' Brendan asked, smiling.

She looked at him with disappointment. She had thought he might have known better. Brendan flinched, mad with himself for letting his relief make him stupid.

'We'll go back to the hospital now to get what I need. Your

friends have offered to get it in the Maternity Hospital – the
Maternity Hospital, I ask you, seems they know someone
there – but I think it's best if I try to get it.' She added, 'Don't
you think?' because Brendan looked wounded.

'They're not my friends. I never met them before,' he said,
and heard how silly that sounded.

'Well, whatever,' the doctor said, raising an eyebrow scepti-
cally, 'back we go.'

Brendan hadn't bargained for this, running around the city
all day in a probably stolen car. But there was nothing for it
now. The doctor didn't speak on the way back. She appeared
preoccupied. Is that window making her cold? he wondered.
Obviously she was running a risk too, he thought.

'Park here,' she said when he reached the gate, and she got
out quickly. Brendan put his hands to his head. Something inside it was thumping wildly. Let this day be over, but sense
told him that fear would only drag it out. He pretended that
he was an ordinary taxi driver. He looked around the car for
something to rub the make-up off his face, the inside of his ear
was tickling, some of it must have trickled into it. He must
look an awful sight. The doctor came out again and almost
skipped in beside him, settling herself in the front seat, holding
a box on her knee.

'Well, so far, so good,' she said.

'Where to, madam?' he said, and she laughed.

He relaxed again. He liked driving, the same way he liked
working. That show of sun was cheerful really, flashing light
on walls that had been hidden by rain for months.

The doctor said, 'The one problem I fear is that it could be
lodged very near the carotid. If that's the case, if I were to slip
even one-eighth of an inch, we'd be in serious trouble . . .'

Brendan shivered and felt himself stiffen again.

'There's a hole on the right side, nasty looking, where the

bullet went in. That can be protected with peroxide. But it's the other side that worries me. I think his bone is sore too, it went right through; it made the hole first and then went right through, hitting the bone along the way, I have no doubt. It's near the surface really, on the left side, half an inch down, that's all, I think. You can feel it if you press hard, although that's difficult because it's very painful for him.'

Brendan could feel his stomach heaving.

'I'll have to get them to agree that if anything goes wrong, if he does start to haemorrhage heavily, they will call an ambulance. Will you do that?'

'If you don't mind, doctor, I'll just do the driving first,' Brendan said. He was glad to have spoken because then he could swallow.

'Oh, you're not going pale on me,' she teased him.

He'd better pull himself together; if he had to stop to vomit on the side of the road, it would surely attract attention. If only she'd stop talking about it. Under his index finger, he could feel the bullet in the man's neck. The skin covering it was hot and purple, ready to burst. Jesus Christ, would this day ever be over?

The doctor helped him find the place this time. When he knocked, the same man came out and pulled the two of them into the kitchen quickly. He seemed more nervous than before. Either the man with the bullet was in worse pain or the strain of waiting here with all the curtains drawn was building up in him. There was the patient now, sitting on a chair, his face white as chalk, pulling at a cigarette, his eyes sunk into pain. The others were crowded around him.

'Did you get the thing?'

'Yes,' the doctor said authoritatively. 'Now, I'll need one of you with me and I think the rest of you should go into another room.'

'Righto,' the oldest man said, 'right.'

'Perhaps you'd like to stay with me?' she said to Brendan.

'Ah no, someone who knows him should be with him,' he said, thinking that up in a flash, out of a reservoir of possible excuses.

The doctor smiled. 'True,' she said.

So the older man opted to stay. The other three and Brendan walked out through the narrow hall to a room opposite.

'What about the ambulance?' the doctor said, as they all tried to crowd through the door together.

'Oh yes.' Brendan stopped and the other three had to stop with him. 'The doctor says that if the man starts to bleed heavily, we'd – you'd – have to get an ambulance immediately.'

They looked at him silently.

'She wants to stress that if you don't promise to do that, then she can't start,' he added, of his own accord. In his heart of hearts he knew that if this went wrong, he wouldn't see these four for lightning; it would be himself and the doctor who would get the man to the hospital. He would stand by her if the worst came to the worst.

'Whatever she says,' the older man said.

Brendan and the three men went into the room. It was empty except for two bare single beds. They sat on them, two to each. Brendan could smell the damp. At least some part of him was still functioning. The men listened intently for the first long minutes. They waited silently for either screams or police cars. When no sound came they lit up cigarettes and started to talk among themselves. They nodded to Brendan every now and again but made no serious attempt to include him, which was just as well, because he had by now set into a frozen lump. Two of the men talked about dog fights, the disgrace they were and more, the blood and guts of them and the cruelty. Brendan said a no-nonsense prayer. The third man suddenly said, 'Anyone want chips?' The other two said that was a good idea. 'Want chips?' he said to Brendan, just a little sneeringly.

'No thanks,' Brendan said, because much and all as he might have liked to please the man, chips were out of the question.

'And a batter burger for me, as well.'

One of them would drive.

'But what if you need the car to get to a phone? If you need an ambulance . . . ?' Brendan asked, as if he hadn't already guessed.

They looked at him, taken aback, all three. 'Oh that, I'm sure we won't,' one of them said.

The doctor tilted the man's head to one side. She injected lignocaine into his neck and, having given it as much time as she could afford, she took out her scalpel. There was not even a millimetre of shaking in her hand. Inside there was a mild flutter, but that could have come from the challenge or the thrill of subterfuge. She told the older man to hold his friend's hand and to talk to him. He did so, closing his eyes and saying that all was going well and looked fine. She cut a perfectly straight line and gently prodded the bullet to the opening. She touched and probed raw flesh and bone; she felt the man go slack under her but she caught his head, let him pass beyond, and dug as far and as often as she needed until she plucked the lead out.

'There,' she said, delight in her voice, holding it in her forceps. 'Now your trouble is over.'

The man came to again and she fed him water. His face was a transparent green and quiet tears ran down his cheeks.

'It is all right,' she said, squeezing his hand and thinking how lucky he – and she – was that she had missed the carotid. She talked to him, then, as she stitched, 'Don't move if you can help it at all.' And he didn't, but she could hear the little sobs coming from his throat. She finished that side. The other was blasted too much, so she would have to protect it as best she could.

'Now for the pain,' she said, patting him on the knee. 'Because I cannot get you to hospital, I will have to sterilise this hole beyond the call of duty.'

His fear began to dart about in shadows on his face, so she decided less talk, more speed. She told him to bear down and to grip the chair. She poured straight solution into his raw flesh. It bubbled like a boiling fizz and she had to say she'd rarely seen a man so brave. The rest was easy. She cleaned and swabbed and dressed. She wrote strict instructions for whoever, wherever, and told him how good he was indeed. He lit a cigarette and pulled on it as if the draw in could make an ordinary day out of this hour.

The doctor came out of the room exactly as the man arrived with the chips. The smell of vinegar met the smell of disinfectant.

'Would you like one?'

'No thank you all the same.'

Brendan and the doctor walked towards town. He was glad to see the end of that car. They were innocent now. At Bewley's in Westmoreland Street she asked him would he like a cup of coffee. He thanked her but said no, he'd better be getting home. They shook hands. As Brendan walked away Rory pulled in beside him. He had the envelope and he drove him home.

Brendan decided to introduce the money in small sums, at particularly bad moments. There is no doubt it would help, quite a lot. He relaxed into the only secret there had ever been between him and Mags.

Some weeks later, alone in the house, he was half-watching the six o'clock news. The reader reported that three men had been charged with armed robbery, Rory was named, and with attempted murder, following a recent shoot-out with *gardaí*. With WHAT? With WHAT?

'It is believed that a fourth man who may have sustained a gunshot wound was also involved *Gardaí* are looking for witnesses and particularly call on any doctor or . . .'

Brendan didn't wait for the nine o'clock news to check. He left a note for Mags saying that he had suddenly got a few days' work around Dundalk and would be in touch the minute he got there. He packed the minimum – he did not want her to notice him seriously gone until the boat had well and truly docked in Liverpool.

When Mags got the letter, she borrowed the fare and arrived on the doorstep of number 52 Durning Street. She was there when Brendan came home from his job on the buildings. His mouth filled up with tears.

She said, 'Will you come home out of that?' She said that nothing might happen to him and if it did they could weather that better than they could weather never seeing him, because you can take one thing for sure, she wasn't coming here to live.

He did come home out of that. Nothing did happen to him, except that he developed a shiver up his back every time he passed Madigan's, or Hynes's, that used to be O'Byrne's.

PARK-GOING DAYS

They took their chairs and children, of whom they were terribly proud today, to the park on the first day of summer, relieved that the darkness was over and repeating again and again 'Great day', so that maybe such sun worship would bring them a summer. You would never have believed that in those few houses there could be so many children – you could easily have forgotten Kathleen's fifth or that Bridie, during the winter, had had another, because, naturally, you never saw it, Bridie's new one, due to the freezing conditions. If you did, Bridie was a bad mother and there were no good or bad mothers around here (even the ones whose sons were inside) – just mothers. It was a Thursday after lunch – the one man who had a job nearby had been fed. No one would have gone to the park before that happened, not in deference to Jack eating, but because Jack's wife wouldn't be free until then, and there was nothing to make a woman feel housebound like all the other women trooping up to the park before her, and there was nothing worse than feeling housebound on a sunny day.

The park-going days of sunshine were truly numbered in this country – fifteen last year, two the year before, ten the year before that and forty on the year that God was otherwise occupied and forgot to switch off the heat, or else decided to tease everyone and make them mournful for the next five years. No woman in this country had any doubt but that God was a man – is a man. There's no was about that fellow unfortunately. Some had the view that the man himself was intrinsically all right and that it was the ones who took over after him who mucked the whole thing up. Could be true – he may have been all right. Perhaps. But it's a hard thing to believe, in a country that only once had forty days of sunshine.

It's amazing the amount of preparations women used to working can put into a trip to the park. One folded-up light deck chair, suntan oil, face cloth, sandwiches (which will avoid having to make a children's tea at six), rug to put sandwiches and children on, sunglasses, small lightish jumpers in case it turns cold suddenly, drinks, the antibiotics that the child is on, some toys for the baby – for the ones who were pregnant last summer – the baby's bottle, one nappy and *all* that baby stuff, *and* ice-cream money.

At ten past two all the doors opened and out they poured, nearly invisible behind all the paraphernalia, calling around them the children who had been dreamy and inside and the ones who had already been outside getting burned and thirsty and cranky. And dirty.

'Look at the face of her. Come here to me until I give you a wipe. Disgracing me.' She dug the face cloth into the child's face, disgracing it in front of friends who hadn't noticed at all.

They went, and Rita went after them. She didn't go to the park but she passed it on the way to the shops, half hoping that if there was a summer next year, or if this one lasted beyond the day, they would ask her to join them, knowing that it would be better if they didn't, because if they ran out of steam – which they would when they realised the sort of her and why – there could be no more casual comments passed between them as strangers. They and she could whistle pleasantries back and forth at the moment; they, prepared to waste their sweet words on her because of curiosity – a new resident – she, to make them less curious, and failing.

The more she said, 'Nice day', the more they wanted to know. The more she felt their sniffing, the more frightened she got. That sneaky-faced woman in the nylon housecoat, too old to walk to the park, polishing her brasses again. Who did she think she was fooling! Of course, she was lonelier than if she was dead, but Rita couldn't be expected to be built of sympathy.

Rita walked after them, aggravated at the bits and pieces of garages built at the ends of gardens, as if thrown together in shapeless anger. In winter she could escape them by looking down at her feet, which she did, but today the sun threw their shadow across the street under her eyes. A bulldozer was needed badly. Knock down the whole lot of them. She had no soft spots for old farm barns, mudwall byres or extended hen houses, so she couldn't see anything for the garages but the bulldozer. Her husband would not have agreed. But then he came from places where fields lay companionably beside other fields that ran casually into more and more fields, flat and hilly, offering space grudgingly to the occasional house, which was then forced to use rickety outhouses as protection against the ever approaching grass. She was from a geometrician's dream, where back gardens were only concessions to the superior needs of houses.

She passed the park and saw them. They belonged to a time before the time of one earring. Two ears, two earrings. Fingers were the only single part of them that divided into ones. They put rings on them. Most importantly, they put one ring on one finger, sometimes along with another, varying in degrees of vulgarity and awfulness. The rings marked stages in their self-denial and destruction. Rita saw the rings glistening in

the sun, picking out unreachable baubles in the sky. The
women saw her and thought different things, none of them
actually about her, more about her type.

'You couldn't satisfy *him*. If it's not the smog, it's the dirt or
the accents. Jayzus, would yeh listen to whose talkin' about an
accent.'

'How *does* she put up with him? An' it's made her odd.'

'There's somethin' else odd about her but I can't put me finger on it.'

'Ah well.'

In the end they knew in their hearts that the only thing
funny about her was that they didn't know her and that she
was married to a culchie. Not much of a gap to be got over.

They settled in their chairs and watched their collective new
generation, comparing it favourably with the other groups in
the park, conscious that they were all part of even more park
groups, between them accounting for hundreds of miles of dis-
carded umbilical cords. They uttered unconnected sentences at
random. Conversation was organised only when there was tragedy or scandal to be related. But the silence was never silent, it
was just a space of time between words of explanation and
words of exasperation.

Bridie watched hers out of the corner of her eye. Sean always dirty. As a baby he sucked the ends of his Babygro and
got a red wrist in his fat little cracks from wet aggravation.
Now he sucked his jumper and pulled at his waist all the time,
ending up each evening with hand marks branded in frustra-
tion on his clothes. His pores seemed to suck in every bit of
street dirt going. His cuts usually went septic. Anne. Wise. Pre-
cocious and clean. She would have children too – it didn't bear
thinking about. She played with her older brothers in a superior bossy way, as if she knew.

'She'll be coming out of school at half two when she makes

her communion, please God.' That would be another step passed in the sending off of her to the Lord.

'It took me all day to get out of town yesterday. Pickets outside the Dáil. They should put that buildin' down the country somewhere and not be stoppin' people tryin' to get home. They wouldn't be so quick to picket it if it was down there.'

They shifted their fat bodies around on the deck chairs. They had suffered from the usual disappointments being married to their husbands. Kathleen's man had been mortified one day when she was nearly due and she'd sat down on the steps of the bank in town, not fit to move another inch. It was a Saturday and the bank was closed – what could he have been going on about?

In her early marriage before having any children, Molly used to call on her husband at work. She thought it was a nice thing to do and she was lonely on her own – she'd been getting eleven pounds before the wedding, now with tax it was only five, so there wasn't much point in her going to work for the short while; the bus fare was two pounds. One day he said that she'd have to stop calling and get used to their new house for both their sakes. The men at work would start talking.

'But I don't know anyone.'

'You'll get to know some mothers later.'

He smiled. She smiled. It was a small subtle exclusion, preparation for the major ones – the tapping on the shoulder as women walked absentmindedly, not deliberately, not provokingly, into supermarkets pushing prams. She never called again.

Bridie's man, when he was young, had kept running from one country to the other, filling himself up with experience, pouring himself all over the Continent and still he hadn't one word to say for himself. He'd only once said 'I love you.' He was a consumer of cultures – he had a few words of French, which gave him an edge on the other men on the street but that was no help to Bridie.

Deirdre's man – the drinker – did his bit for his children. He talked about them occasionally in pubs in the serious way that drunk men do, once getting first-day issue stamps for them from a man who worked in the P & T, who happened, just happened, to be drinking beside him. Now that was more than a woman could do.

Kathleen had broken her mother's heart – 'Ma, I wasn't going to tell you this but seeing we're out for the day and that it's on my mind and I have been keeping it to myself and all that and it's no good for me or anything and all that and no good for you either and I'm pregnant.'

Kathleen sighed. Bridie put her varicose veins on the wheel of the pram. These – the fat, the veins, the sighs – were the shapes of the backbone of the country. You'd never think it to see the corkscrew, frown-free pictures that poured from the ad men's anorexic fantasies.

'Great day.'

'A doctor said to my mother once that there are two terrible bad things for a woman – ironing and not dropping everything to run outside when she sees the first blink of sun.'

'Yeah, it's a great day.'

'I'd love a cigarette. Funny the way you feel like it sometimes and not at others.'

'I didn't know you smoked, Molly.'

Molly raised her voice to panic pitch. 'Smoke. Smoke is it? I was a chain-smoker. What! I had meself burnt. Me lips, me skirts, me bras, me slips. One match would do me the whole day. Lit one off the other.'

'What did you smoke?' It was neither a question nor a statement after Molly's emotion.

'Albany.'

'Were they a special cigarette, I don't remember them? I used to smoke Woodbine. No one ever died that smoked Woodbine.'

'It's near tea time.'

That was a grand day. No one had got cut or desperately badly hurt. There had been the odd row but not enough to deserve a beating. One woman, not belonging to their group, had set her child up for a battering. She hit her because she wanted to go on the swings too often. The child kicked her back. The women nodded a sort of ungrudging, serve-you-right nod. The mother hit her more. The incident might have spiralled into murder but the floating disapproval, the soul sympathy, and the take-it-easy-it'll-get-better thoughts made the mother acknowledge defeat. Yes, a great day.

They were gathering up their stuff when Rita walked past, on her way home. They delayed, to let her go on. They were sick of her kind, really – never any children, coming to live in that rented house, teasing their curiosity and staying aloof.

'You wouldn't mind so much marrying a culchie but getting *used* to him.'

They laughed. They could have remarked that she was unhappy but they denied her that status, in the mean way that city people can, surrounded as they are by so many, some of whom, precisely because of the number, are dispensable. They turned their noses up and pulled their curtains down an inch from their faces like country ones could never do. (Perhaps you might need your neighbour in twenty years when all the rest would be gone, to America, or Dublin.)

As they struggled nearer their doors, exhausted from heat, children whingeing when *they* saw the prospect of home looming closer, that they hadn't stayed long enough in the park, only three hours, Mammy, they each withdrew themselves from collective experience and concentrated on their individual problems. Parks were all right – open-air sum totals of lives that were normally lived in box rooms with thick enough doors and walls to shut out obscenities – but all the same, you wouldn't want to live in a park all your life and you wouldn't want to behave in your own house as if you were in a park. After a while people get on your nerves, even on sunny days – that was why the tenants in the rented house were always handy. Everyone on the street could take their mutual spite out on them and so avoid major street fights.

Rita knew what they were thinking. Sometimes at four in the morning – she often woke at four – she would look out and see reflections of their lights and she would feel like forgiving them because who couldn't forgive a woman anything when they saw her struggling at that unearthly hour to silence a crying, hungry baby? Rita had had a child of her own. The child had died and she wasn't allowed to think about it. What had happened was anyone's guess – it just died. But Rita was fine now. Fine. The street would have gushed with sympathy if it had known. One thing Rita regretted not having was park days with mothers. She'd noticed the way mothers made up to the children on park days. Made up to them for all sorts of troubles, things like concentrated, compressed family violences that emptied onto children's backsides when men and women decided at the same moment that they would have to put manners on the offspring who was at that second holding their nerves to ransom. They could do that because they knew that mothers would make it up sometime soon – certainly in a park if it was a sunny day. Rita would have liked the making-up bits.

It was Bridie in the end who asked Rita if she wanted to sit down with them in the park, just for a few minutes, for a little rest. Rita stretched her legs out in front of her and said to herself, now I'll have to leave. They talked busily as they watched the replay of yesterday and yesterday. Rita not thinking all the time of her own because she wasn't allowed to; each of the other women remarking to herself how nice she was really. The next day it rained. Clouds stalked over the bit of sunshine they'd had and Rita started packing. She said goodbye before herself and her culchie husband left, knocked on the single doors and got away before they learned anything about her. A week later if you could have cut bits out of the walls, you would have seen them cleaning noses, swiping at bare legs, sneaking off for a rest and drying clothes, bending over babies in the way that causes bad backs, again, again, as the tenants moved in and the rain poured on them all.

THE LAST CONFESSION

I swear to you, she was absolutely normal. Is absolutely normal. If I tell you a little about our childhood and how normal we were, and if I don't tell you until later what she actually did, you'll say that I cheated you into thinking that she was normal, but then, if I tell you first, you'll think of her as the person who did what she did and you won't take in just how normal she was. Is. I argue this out with myself a lot, will I think about her today as she was, or is that fooling myself? Or will I think about the mess she has created for me, all of us, herself? But then that is denying the fact, the truth, that she is a perfectly normal woman.

My sister. I am three years older than her, there are the two of us. I was adored because I was the boy; she, because she was the girl. We adored each other, maybe I adored her a little more than she did me because she took streaks of the sun with her into rooms even in wintertime. We talked lots, we liked to tease each other. That's an odd way of looking at it, we loved to tell each other, although we only said that so the other person would say it back. We loved the idea that we might be odd. There wasn't a hope in hell. Sometimes when she did things that I had just done I wanted to say copycat because I felt that I had nothing of my own – my mother, when telling stories to the neighbours, would even mix up which of us had said what – but I didn't dare because I was afraid to hurt her, and anyway, there were advantages – if what I was doing and saying was worth copying, then I was making my presence felt, wasn't I?

Other times, when I would suggest doing something daring, like jumping from the top of the hay on to the barn floor, she would say, 'Yes, you've talked me into it', although I wouldn't have tried persuasion at all. She sometimes used sentences like that, just to see how her saying them sounded, they were such un-Irish sentences, sentences that were being thrown about in movies, but we had no movies in Monaghan. Where she could have learned them, I don't know. She was much quicker than me at things like that, picking up words, ideas. Particularly when the sun shone. Later she told me this was because she's Aquarian but I let that pass. I felt it was just the light. A day when the road was dry, it was even white, the sun lit the whole way down it, 'burned' would be too strong a word, you could imagine that there was dust in the air it was so hot, although this would have been a gross exaggeration. Our shadows were there in front of us – remnants of the dark winter just gone – we danced on top of each other's until we got irritated because we could never dance on our own. Or get rid of it. We made them walk up hedges. Actually this shadow-dancing served more than one purpose. If we were really annoyed, we could screw our heels viciously into each other's heads, and pretend it was a joke. One time she merged our shadows into one. She made me promise never to fall out with her. It wasn't hard to make me do that, I had no intentions of it.

For a while, when she was thirteen and I was sixteen, our friendship changed. She still loved me but I spent my time trying to impress her, which is not love. I thought it was, but now know better. After a time, I gave that nonsense up and went back to being her real friend. She seemed to have learned a lot; she talked even more than before. I couldn't keep up with her – even normally I cannot talk and think at the same time. I have to think it out first and then I forget it when it comes to talking if I'm not given a long time to say it slowly. I bite the inside of my mouth with agitation at times like this. But she could talk and think and also draw my attention to the fact that the inside of my mouth would end up in ridges if I didn't stop that, which only made me worse.

But with all this talking she could still figure things out – as I said, she could talk and think together. She always made me feel as if I was following her, when I know that wasn't really true. But I had to hand it to her, when I grew my hair half an inch below my collar she fought for me day and night. She fought so long and hard with our parents that you'd think she was the one who had offended the rules. ('Rules' is too mild a word, so, too, is 'way of life'.) And yet, even when she was fighting with them, for herself now, too, about the length of her skirts, she could defend them to me. I said, out of their hearing, of course, that if they both stopped smoking there'd be more money for clothes for us and wasn't it their duty? She said no, that parents also had rights of their own and they were entitled to their cigarettes if they wanted to kill themselves. On the subject of which she never liked to linger. Part of the work of maturing involved forcing yourself to be interested in who that was who died yesterday, who they were related to, what age they were and what killed them. But she would have none of this, she said that there was more to life than dying and she had better things to be thinking about. She said once that she loathed the way people said, 'Do you know what I think is very sad?' with delight and glee in their voices. Really loathed it. I remember the day she said that. I should have believed myself and known that that day was as monumental as I thought it was, us standing there with one foot each against the wall, discussing death, life and love. I should have believed myself. I could have enjoyed it, too, because life was not so complicated then.

I went to a new city – I should say, I went to a city. I still sometimes remember the pride of daily arriving in the right street, the attention I gave to details that I cannot now see (I cannot even recall what the details were), the feeling that my life was one long, undeserved festival. But I missed some things, my sister mostly. She passed through my flat on her way to her new city. We talked nearly all night. She asked me did I ever hear the way when one person says to another, 'I can't stand such and such' or 'I hate when . . .' or 'I wouldn't have that . . .' and the other person says, 'I'm the same'? She said she always felt like saying, Well, I'm not. We also talked about losing our faith. Everyone talked about that at the time, and how wonderful it was to be rid of all that hypocrisy. It was a lovely night and I saw her off the next morning, excited for her, she was so delighted.

She spent five years away. I lived an ordinary life and, I suppose, missing her sharpness, I slipped and let it become more ordinary than it had to be. By the time she came home I had become certain that I knew everything I needed to know. I was solid. And I think we had lost our unconditional love. We talked to, not with, each other. But we still loved each other. Maybe I was a little afraid of her because she had stayed faithful to the overwhelming wonder that we had had when we were young. I couldn't stand the incessantness of that wonder. She would sit down, ready to talk for hours about something political – not just ready, compelled, it was our duty, our lives. I felt that it was one big fairly empty game, someone else's, things were and would be. She looked at me sadly but took it in her stride and then started talking about our personal lives.

She could still do that too. My unconditional love came back.

When I told her that I was getting married, she said that personally she found marriage obscene. It was built on men owning women. I said it worked both ways. She said, 'Like hell it does and you know it.' She narrowed her eyes and lips closer together than I'd ever seen them. I knew, if I was truthful to myself, that she had a point but I wanted a private place in which to have my worries, a place where I could break down without being seen or remarked upon.

She came to the wedding and was the most gracious sister-in-law I have ever seen, wishing my now wife every good that she could imagine, fearful for her, even though it was me that was the husband! I was very torn, for a second, when it came to getting into the going-away car, knowing that she somehow felt disappointed in me, but you can imagine which side I took – it's not every day you get married. As my wife and I pulled away (embarrassed by such ancient innuendo and really us nearly tired looking at each other naked), she put on a superior look, but I knew that she didn't mean it, it was just defence against isolation.

Ah yes, it had been a long five years, the longest.

About a year after that, I got the strangest request. I was asked to come to the Bishop's Palace in Drumcondra, on the Drumcondra Road, nearly opposite where the Lemon's Sweet Factory was, still is, but nobody works in it now, so I suppose you wouldn't really call it a factory. There was an embossed shield on the notepaper, although the envelope was plain. I jokingly said to my wife, 'You haven't filed for an annulment have you?' I was at a loss to know what on earth it could be about, but they very politely wouldn't tell me over the phone, yet they nearly begged me to turn up. There was no fear that I wouldn't, because my curiosity was well and truly whetted.

When I reached the gate I started getting nervous, it was like being called to account for all your movements, your sins, before you had died. I have always believed that I will be able to manage a reasonable number of excuses – that is, if there's a God, you understand – on the actual day itself, death will have given me a new maturity, but to have to do it before dying, I wasn't prepared for that. I had never been at the gates before – well, it's not the sort of place that you can be at. It's just there, a looming gate that somehow swallows you.

Actually, I tell a lie. I had been there once. I had arranged to meet my sister for a drink on a February night that had been night all day. She rang me at work and said, very fast, that she would be at a picket outside the Bishop's Palace and could I pick her up there. See you. So I had to go. When I arrived more snow had fallen, it vainly tried to look white. It was so cold I could have cried. But the women were cheerful; they were up against such odds they laughed a lot. More than me, I had to admit, who was happier. I presumed. She was like a ball of ice when she got into the car, but a few hot whiskeys and she said she was thawed out. I wasn't, but I let it go. Then I said, 'Would you like another drink somewhere nicer?' And she said delightedly, 'Yes, as long as it's in Dún Laoghaire, at the North Wall docks or the airport.'

Well, I was further than the gate this time. The avenue is, quite simply, frightening. I mustn't be the first person to think this, because after Vatican Two, they cut down trees leading up to lots of chapel gates so that people would feel more part of the whole thing. Less frightened. When I think about that day, I dwell on my reactions to the avenue because they were the most and the least important.

The bishop said that there was a problem with my sister and could I tell him something about her. I said tersely, 'I beg your pardon', meaning, who the *hell* do you think you are and *what* in God's name do you take me for? He then said, 'We thought it would be best to speak to you rather than your parents.' I said, '*Sorry?*', meaning, are you threatening me? (In the circumstances this was a bit premature of me.) He said, 'To get to the point quickly, your sister is threatening us. She has forged some photographs of a few individual priests, in compromising positions; she says she is going to release them to the newspapers. We cannot, of course, allow that. And will not,' he added. 'Perhaps you can help us. I realise this must come as a shock to you, I'm sure you didn't know the character of your sister' – I feebly thought, Who does this geezer think he is? – 'So I will leave it with you until tomorrow.' But I don't know where she is, I thought, already following orders. I was being dismissed.

When I got outside the door I had a splitting headache. If I could have got my hands on her throat! But then I smiled, just briefly. One evening we had exchanged notions of uncomfortable moments.

'You know, when you hop into the front of a taxi by mistake and the minute you're in there you realise you've done the wrong thing and you want to say to the driver, Sorry, I thought it was my own car, but you say nothing and he says nothing and you stare out the window and wish to God the journey was over. You even contemplate climbing into the back seat but that would make it worse. I hate that.'

'Last week I was at this traditional music singing session, proper traditional, and the man beside me started to sing "The Wild Rover" and everyone turned to glare and I wanted to jump up and say, He's not with me, honestly, I swear he's not.'

'Or the doctor intimates to you to take off your clothes and get on the couch, you strip naked, he turns around and says, "I only meant your skirt", you blush to a temperature of one hundred and four degrees and he says, "But it's all right if you're happy." God, you feel like a flasher of the lowest order, taking advantage of a doctor.'

'Worse than that, I was beside a bank robber one day. Every time I go into the bank now I want to say, Look, see me, I'm not a bank robber, I was only beside him.'

Bad moments. Well, this one beats them all.

I sweated for a week, day and night, and had the most terrible dreams day and night. The bishop was in constant contact. It put a strain on my marriage. My wife said that it was one thing being a Catholic but quite another having the bishop ring you up every day. It put her off the normal business of living, she said. It certainly changed the atmosphere in our bedroom. Then my sister rang, as they had guessed she would, oh, they always know.

She told me that she'd had a great laugh today because this old man beside her on the bus had blessed himself halfway up the Rathmines Road. So she was in Dublin, well, I knew that anyway from the money dropping in. She told him she thought it was a good idea. He said, chuffed, 'Blessing yourself passing the chapel? Yes.' She said, 'Oh I didn't know it was the church, I thought you were blessing yourself passing the Battered Women's Centre.'

'Shut up,' I screamed at her, 'what the hell do you think you're at?' God, how I wished for simplicity just at that minute. I didn't want to know why she had done it. I didn't want to have to make any connections, I just wanted to know what to do next, and I was glad that she was all right.

She said, 'Do you remember the party where we all discussed our last confessions?' Yes, I remembered. I had waited at the edge of their talk, a sound that was growing in excitement every minute – I must admit some of them were funny – 'Please Father, I broke the fifth commandment', she had meant to say that she had committed adultery. Afterwards she thought how could he be so calm when he thought she'd killed somebody and she just knew that he wouldn't have taken it so easily if she had got her commandment right. It set her to thinking. Then another voice said, 'I said, "Please Father, I've been heavy petting" – what, by the way, *does* heavy petting mean? – he asked me was I going to marry the man and I nearly jumped out of my skin. "Well, give him up then." It was easier to give up the confessions.' And the usual tales of the probing priest: And what do you mean by that? And what does he do? And do you take pleasure out of it? I waited so I could tell mine. It was a good one. They all laughed. But I left them. I had only wanted to say it, not get involved. They were taking it too seriously. They seemed to be making out of the conversation a collective harm done to them. And maybe it was, because, after all, my humiliation was not as thorough, the priest was a man. Yes, I remembered. 'Well, I got the idea then,' she said. She would take revenge.

And so she tricked three priests, four actually – how many? I moaned – maybe half a dozen. It was easy. She photographed them afterwards when they were asleep, pulled the sheets back and photographed them. She described some of them, their confessions to her, the photos, asking someone to take a photo-graph of her and one of them without him seeing. Wasn't that dicey? But by then she was as high as a kite on what she was going to do. She said she was doing it to blow apart the *total* hypocrisy – 'I mean TOTAL' – and I got impatient thinking, Yes, yes, yes, but you can't do that. I then said, 'But didn't it bother you, sleeping with priests?' 'Yuk,' she said, and added that it wasn't only men who could enjoy revenge.

She wouldn't see me. 'Oh please, just so I can talk some sense into you.' No, no, she wouldn't. So they were wrong about that, they said that she would definitely see me.

The following Saturday's papers carried a note to the effect that the photographs existed, an unsigned statement from my sister saying she had no objections to priests having sexual relationships as long as they didn't pretend that they weren't and as long as they admitted it openly and changed the laws accordingly and were as generous to everybody else and stopped fooling the people, etc., etc. The bishops also had a statement about a blackmail note from some nutcase who had constructed a number of photographs she alleged were of priests. They didn't know who she was and preferred to let the matter rest. Didn't know who she was, hah!

Well, how come next morning there were police cars everywhere around our street? They stayed there for a month, so soon the neighbours had the whole story. The *gardaí* told them, in order to relieve their boredom and get them on their side. It was unbearable. So we sold our house and moved out here to the wilderness. The neighbours don't see the police cars, there are no neighbours.

My wife doesn't talk about my sister. Neither do I. But oh, I do love to think about her often, sometimes, like now.

ESCAPING THE
CELTIC TIGER, WORLD MUSIC
AND THE MILLENNIUM

Anne Marie McGurran was driven demented by the mention of three things, the Celtic Tiger, World Music and the Millennium. She had been seen punching her fist at the sky, in a way that could not be mistaken for the action of someone at a rock concert or Croke Park. She had been seen, in riveting company, with her forehead in one hand and using the other to actually pull out single hairs. She had been heard. Oh, she had been heard.

What were they, these words that crackled her head and amplified her voice up into a half-strangled screech? One was a bad, really bad, two words that had slipped off the tongue of some wiggling economist, more or less at the same time as three fellows were sitting in a pub in London making up the two words World Music. WM was for pale-faced people who didn't like the sound of folk, too florid, or ethnic, too thorny. And also for lazy people who couldn't be bothered distinguishing between Bulgaria and the Andes. CT was for speedy people who needed a smokescreen, behind which to hide the poor mean lives that were still being lived on the terraces, despite the New Financial Centre, coloured mobile phones and exploding property prices. The Millennium was a made-up date that frightened her and put terrible pressure on her with regard to what part of the country or the world she should be in when the clock struck twelve.

Why was she worried about words? What had they got to do with her? Hadn't people eventually stopped saying 'excellent' every time they had a cup of watery tea, stopped, without any intervention by herself. What was her problem? She wasn't writing a dictionary. There are people who would not have thought that these words were crucial in any way, would indeed have regarded thinking about them as an affectation, but for Anne Marie McGurran they were a matter of life or death. Or at least a matter of the difference between walking straight-backed and hanging over the edge of the road, blinded by a private row with lexicology. Life or death, in other words. She had recently returned to the old sod – more words that had been dropped from the new lingo, too rural, too muddy. It was essential that she wriggle herself into some measure of comfort with current expression, otherwise she would have to flee again, and this time she was trying to plant her feet for a while to see what would sprout. And so she was trying to pacify her aggravation.

When still young, she had spent a lot of time wondering about what job she would do.

'I want to be a nun.'

'No, you don't.'

'I want to be a priest.'

'No, you can't.'

'I want to be a mother.'

'That's not a job.'

'A doctor then.'

'Your aunt's a nurse.'

'A sailor.'

'Oh, for God's sake.'

'Mammy, how come the sea is deeper in some places? It's not as if someone built it.'

'I'll go gather up those fallen leaves.'

That was her father who said that – he'd let her mother bloody well answer that last question. He was a man who left a lot to his wife but bought her plenty of jewellery.

Her cousins came from America. They weren't allowed to watch the news – too much violence and disaster. If there wasn't one on at the minute, the news did anniversaries of mass shootings. Anne Marie's house would be a funny place if no one watched the news. Maybe she'd go to America, such difference could only be good. Her cousins, who were still young, thought that if you wanted to be president, you could. Even without the news. She was still at 'Forgive me, Father, I am not worthy'.

'I want to be taoiseach.'

'We're not even *in* Fianna Fáil.'

Anne Marie left and followed jobs around the world, cleaning toilets on two continents, waiting on tables in America – my name is Anne Marie, if you need me just call, is everything all right? You want the dessert menu, that seems like a good plan. She chiselled gargoyles in Queensland University, no worries. She was able to take things as philosophically as the next person from her island, having fitted into the wash of a history that included starvation, loss of tongue, being shot off fields and crushed on to boats that would dock in America or Australia if their creaky bottoms survived the high seas. The job she really wanted was to flag landing planes into their parking spots but she couldn't discover the training requirements.

Anne Marie became a learned journeyer, able to take her countries as they came, able to shift into the gears of talk from Kansas to Kathmandu. She carried her life with her the way travellers handle luggage. She watched them dragging bags when they were tired, too exhausted for words. Well-slept by morning, they picked them up like butterflies, seeing a full summer in every single beam of light, every solitary lark. Her suitcase became her life. Her heart was in it.

But gradually she began to miss a tone of voice. It looked as if she would have to go home; find out if it was safe. It would be good to hurry past people going to the tourist office in her own town.

Before leaving, she called on old friends.

'You can't change the world, only yourself.'

'Not if you decide that you can't change the world and would prefer to think only of yourself.'

'No, it's more important to change yourself. Stop smoking. You cause less pollution, so it does do something for the common good.'

'Bullshit.'

'I think it's time you went home.'

'I'm going.'

Her old friends were healing the politics out of themselves. She spoke to a Catholic about this.

'I'm at a loss to know what to think,' he said.

When she was small she found out that there were two ways of getting attention, being sick or missing. She then learned which was the most attractive of the two. Being sick brought kind words, a lot of hot tea and tucking in of clothes, as if she was being parcelled up to be sent somewhere. Being missing had more fringe benefits. But after a time they were pointless, because she wasn't there to enjoy them. All these thoughts were dress rehearsals for re-entry.

At first it was holidays on wheels. The days were clear.

'There doesn't seem to be as much rain as I remember.'

People smiled at that, behind her back. They didn't always

catch her eye, with good reason. The days were linenfresh. The people who had stayed behind had fought the fight and hauled the country up, making it into a grown-up place. They weren't always fond of those who had been having long cock-tails beside swimming pools, while they were stamping their feet on demonstration lines that were frozen solid, making the participants almost a single unit. This was one reason that they didn't always catch her eye. Her past friends sifted through her. Some of them now had power and could hurt her with it. But others led her back onto the first steps and in no time at all she was complaining with familiarity, in intimate chorus with the rest of them.

That was ages ago, a half year or so.

At the make-up counter in Arnott's the women were dis-cussing, out loud,without shame, the hiding of lines. Maybe it had always been so. But what happened next hadn't. A couple were kissing on Anne Marie's street corner, deep kissing in the way that doesn't happen on streets now, because people have places to go and the promise of more is not withheld. They were good kissers, the right height for it, and their mouths moved smoothly in time, like dancers taking the cor-ners well. Anne Marie was glad. Then the man's mobile phone rang. He put his hand into his pocket.

'You can't do that,' Anne Marie screamed. 'Keep kissing.'

The couple stared at her.

'Take your call,' the woman said, because the thought of someone like Anne Marie was a dangerous thought.

And then that evening in Hughes's, from among the regu-lars, that pile of stories in the corner, were heard the words World Music. Followed by Celtic Tiger and Millennium. The man and woman who said them had identical straight smiles, like the two ends of a zipper that would fit into each other. Anne Marie stopped in her tracks on the way to the bar. Her life had become her own by virtue of the worry that she had invested in it. And the kinds of worry. She had retained a division in her worries – home and street. The danger was in the collision. But that could mostly be avoided. It was a matter of shaping her thoughts so that when she was out they were contained, not spilling all over her face and conversation. But those words! Those words! And not from a radio when one was at home washing dishes and could beat the wall. Being used out in a pub! And in Hughes's! Still, here's a thing. If she could put them together, see them as isolated pestilence, words with no connotations, and ignore them . . . If she could ignore them, her life could take on the new meaning that had been missing for so many months it was almost a year. She needed new meanings regularly. She didn't care how they came, the sun of a day, remembering a squirrel, or a long straight road, a kiss that was meant. And there in that moment, frozen stiff, mesmerised, halfway to the bar, where she could be run over if she didn't move, she tried to stop the panic of not belonging, of being ousted by words. She would have to make her mind up about what to do

She could stay. Last week she'd met a man who was on the sidelines. The surprise of the minor, but continuous, bad luck of his life was in his eyes. And now his neighbours' children were making huge money, while he still couldn't afford even a banger of a car. When they were out walking he had picked up a bird's feather and given it to her. Not the sort of thing that can be easily forgotten. If he told her he loved her, what would she do? It always surprised her how the sound of that sentence changes the view. If she married him, she thought that they would shake hands at their wedding. So she could stay, to see what might happen. But the man walked into the pub and Anne Marie was filled with regret because, looking at him, she suddenly knew that no statement of his could make up

for those other new words, whose creation had made her forever a stranger in the place that she had, with too much confidence, called home. And the idea of trying to explain was even
worse than the thought. Here, on the way to the bar, she had a
sudden warm vision of her suitcase. She raised her fist to the
sky. It was time to find a new desert within which to put her
heart.